ABOUT THE AUTHOR

Kevin Bruce is a native Californian born in San Francisco in 1941. He has been engaged in many professions, working variously as a musician, Russian interpreter, advertising copywriter, and real estate appraiser. He received a bachelor's degree in business from the University of Nebraska, Omaha, in 1968 and more recently a Master of Liberal Arts degree from Stanford University in 1999. His master's thesis evolved into his first book, *The Murals of John Pugh: Beyond Trompe L'Oeil*, published in 2005. His second book, *Large Art in Small Places – discovering the California mural towns*, was published in 2009. Both are published by Ten Speed Press/Random House. He is currently engaged as an author and an art historian with a focus on chronicling the contemporary mural. He resides with his wife Pauline in Scottsdale and Star Valley, Arizona. His father was J. Campbell Bruce, author of *Escape from Alcatraz*, the basis for the movie of the same name, and the inspiration for this novel.

BOOKS BY KEVIN BRUCE

Non-fiction

The Murals of John Pugh - Beyond Trompe L'Oeil

Large Art in Small Places - discovering the California mural towns

Both published by Ten Speed Press/Random House.

Fiction

AFTER ALCATRAZ - surviving the escape
(Formerly titled: Still Water … after the escape from Alcatraz)

Both published by Trifoil Press

After ALCATRAZ

surviving the escape

Kevin Bruce

ISBN-13:
978-0692608524 (Trifoil Press)

ISBN-10:
0692608524

DEDICATION

To Ken Gunderson whose enthusiasm and encouragement set me on the path to this book; and to Pauline who kept me there.

ACKNOWLEDGEMENTS

Thanks to everyone who helped me with this project: my wife, for her sound advice and editing, my brother Anthony and my sister Lisa, my cousin Scotty and his wife Jill, and my daughter Kelly. And especially to my friends Ken and Kelly Gunderson who really helped in the research and the beginnings of this book.

Without their help and encouragement, this book would probably still be in bits and pieces in a big manila envelope in my desk drawer.

PROLOGUE .... JUNE 1962, ALCATRAZ

From the small rocky shore nothing can be seen but dark water and an occasional wisp of fog. The scene is intermittently lit by short flashes of light that are high over the heads of three men facing the water. They are struggling with a makeshift raft made of some sort of inflatable plastic and several boards. Behind them is a steep hill and on the hill are the dark walls of a fortress-like structure. Atop a tall tower on the closest corner of the wall is a revolving light. The three men place the raft into the water and push off, hanging onto the sides and quietly kicking their feet. They slowly disappear into the night. The intermittent light is all that is left of this curious tableau.

CHAPTER ONE ... JUNE 1962, THE BAY

Three men slip off the Rock and into the dark waters of the San Francisco Bay on the night of June 11, 1962. The plan is to head for Angel Island, the closest land to Alcatraz, and then north from there. They have crude backpacks with a few dollars they've saved and some civilian clothes they had fashioned out of scraps that were swiped from the clothing shop where two of the men, the Anglin brothers, had worked on Alcatraz. They are pushing a makeshift raft made out of inflated raincoats that had been hand stitched and glued together, and the seams vulcanized on exposed steam pipes in the utility corridor behind their cells.

After a short while in the water they get into an argument in the middle of the bay. The two brothers want to deviate from the plan and head straight toward the alluring lights of San Francisco. They are so close it seems like the easiest point of land to get to. Easiest is not always best but the Anglin brothers don't buy that.

It was never in the plan to swim to San Francisco; too many people; too many cops. But the other man, Frank Morris, lets them go without an argument. He figures he can make better time if he is alone. They separate and Frank thinks "good riddance". He takes the raft as he appears to be furthest from landfall. In actuality, he is fairly close to Angel Island.

The Anglins, after a concentrated effort at swimming as effortlessly as possible, come upon an old freighter moored to a dark and otherwise deserted pier.

The brothers climb up the mooring line of the ship and stow away in an abandoned paint locker in the bow. They are not spotted, as the ship is not under any sort of watch due to the fact that the crew is short by two men.

They settle down in the dark locker and soon the engines begin to vibrate and they can sense the ship is getting underway. They fitfully rest as the ship moves through the Bay and out through the Golden Gate. But after a while the ship, which has been moving slowly up to this point, picks up speed and really begins to move around. Their hiding place is getting too much like a roller coaster to handle so they carefully open the door and step out onto the moving deck. The brothers have never been on any boat bigger than the one that took them out to Alcatraz several years back. They don't see anything but water around them. The land is gone. And they are a little queasy, or maybe a lot queasy. It's hard to tell. They are heading for the heaving rail in case they have to throw up when they feel a tap on their shoulders. They've been caught, and by a tall, giant of a man. They are in no shape to resist and where would they go anyway.   They march down the deck and up some stairs and are delivered to the Captain on the bridge.

The Captain is not completely shocked by their presence. He surmises that they are the two brothers who had escaped from Alcatraz in the night and who were the subject of a call from the Coast Guard earlier. At the time of the call he was not aware of their presence on board and told the Coast Guard that he had never seen them, which, at the time, was true. But when they are brought to him he puts two and two together and realizes he has two captive crew candidates that are greatly in his debt and will work for next to nothing. He doesn't bother to tell them about the Coast Guard call or that he knows who they are. He welcomes them on board as they enter international waters headed for the far-east.

Frank Morris is swimming towards Angel Island pushing the raft and using his home-made life vest for further flotation. The water is cold; bone chilling cold. Fortunately, the tide is changing so the pull is neutral for the moment. The sky is dark with occasional wisps of fog. He is low in the water and from this vantage point everything seems farther away. He can see the lights of the North and East Bay and a large dark area where they disappear. He can only guess that this is the bulk of Angel Island blocking out the light. He is swimming steadily. He occasionally flips over on his side to give himself a breather. And then back onto his belly where he swims with an ungainly one-armed version of the Australian crawl holding on to the raft with one hand. But he is slowly making headway. The blackness of the island is getting bigger and he can only see the lights to the north in his peripheral vision.

And then disaster strikes. He is struck with almost crippling leg cramps. It is all he can do to keep swimming with his arms. His legs are useless; and incredibly painful. He can only move them with great effort. Thank God for the raft.

Just when he is sure that he can't swim another stroke a miracle occurs. His knees hit the pebbles on the bottom and he is all at once surrounded by the mild surf lapping at the edge of the island. He has made it to land; even if he still is on an island; and still in the bay. He pulls himself on shore and massages his aching legs. They respond to his ministrations and he can finally stand. He carefully heads north along the shoreline around Angel Island to the eastern shore closest to the lights of the East Bay.

Frank rethinks his strategy. Marin County is sort of a dead end and you'd need to head east to really put some distance between you and the inevitable hordes of searchers that are sure to come. Also, the original plan was to steal a car and ride south or east. But that was when he was still hobbled with the Anglins. Now he is not so sure. A car theft will not go unnoticed. It will leave a trail. The authorities would expect him to go north to Marin just like they had planned. But he now has other ideas. Maybe he should head east. He walks to the north of the island keeping close to the shore so as not to leave a trail. Maybe his pursuers will think the three of them are still together.

He heads to the eastern shore of the island. Although it is a longer swim to the East Bay, he believes there are train tracks close to the water, between the breakwater and the north-south highway on the mainland. If he can get to them he might be able to hop a freight. He'd done that a couple of times in his youth and he just might be able to do it again. All he has to do is get back into the freezing water and take another little swim. At least this time he is alone; and glad of it. With the noisy brothers gone he feels he has a better chance to slip away from the San Francisco Bay area unnoticed.

So with a new-found confidence he enters the water and begins his final swim. The tide is coming in which will be a big help, especially with the raft. He has farther to go; much longer but easier.

He climbs up onto the raft and pushes off. The lights of the East Bay cities act as welcoming beacons and for the first time since he entered the waters off of Alcatraz he feels he just might succeed.

At least, he thinks, he'll get to dry land. He hopes the rest will work itself out. He'll deal with what happens next when the time comes. If he wasn't so damn cold, he would have a better chance. But what the hell, the chances of getting off of the Rock were next to nothing and here he is swimming for the mainland. He is sure he can make it if he just keeps putting one arm in front of the other. And so he does.

When he finally reaches the large slippery rocks of the breakwater he is silently ecstatic. He's made it. He stows the raft between two large rocks. (It will drift off the rocks at high tide and eventually end up on the shore of Angel Island leading the authorities to conclude that it was abandoned in the bay and that the escaped prisoners are dead.) Frank carefully navigates the breakwater rocks and walks in a low crouch up to an eight-foot chain-link fence. After the walls and fences of Alcatraz this one is a joke. He scrambles over. On the other side of the fence he discovers that he is in an open area with the north-south freeway not too far away. He makes his way carefully across the open ground to the edge of the freeway. His doesn't find any railroad tracks. Maybe they are on the other side of the freeway. But how does he get across? He can't run across it. It is very wide and he would surely be noticed; if not run over.

He walks north, parallel to the freeway, hoping to find a way to the other side. He is sheltered from the traffic by oleander bushes that are planted along the edge of the freeway. When he is about to turn around and go in the other direction he spots a culvert that appears to run under the freeway. He enters the culvert on his hands and knees and makes his way through the mess of bottles and debris at the entrance. He keeps moving. It is eerie to hear and feel the cars going overhead. He finally reaches the end of the culvert and emerges into another open area. After that long crawl he finds it is hard to stand up. He's getting old on top of all of his other troubles. He begins walking away from the freeway and in a short time he sees, in the very near distance, just what he has hoped for. There are railroad tracks. He makes his way to the tracks and he decides it must be the main north-south line. He hunkers down between two bushes on the edge of a fence to wait for a train. While he waits, he takes stock of his situation. He has his waterproof pouch under what is left of his prison garb. It contains his fresh shirt. It also contains a little money he saved from the actual cash they paid out for all of his long hours of work on the rock. His cash on hand comes to under five bucks. The rest of his earnings were credited to his work account. Maybe he would write and ask for them. Probably not.

He is beginning to have serious doubts about his train-trip plans when he sees a light in the distance on the north-bound track. He hopes it is a freight train and not one full of passengers. The light grows steadily larger and soon he can hear the sound of the diesel engines. They are pulling what appears to be a very long freight train. But it is picking up speed. Frank realizes he probably has only one chance to find a car with an open door, to run alongside of it, and pull himself inside before the increasing speed of the train makes that impossible. But no open doors are to be found.

He is just about to settle on climbing up the rungs on the side of a tank car and trying to travel that way, in the open, when he spots a boxcar with one of the doors about a quarter of the way open. He hopes he can fit in that space. He runs next to the train, grabs the edge of the door frame, and makes a lunge at the opening. With his last ounce of strength, he launches himself into the dark interior of the car. He is safe; at least for a while. And most importantly he is moving away from San Francisco at a fairly good clip. He leans up against the side of the car and immediately falls asleep. He is completely exhausted.

The train moves north and then, at last, turns east toward Sacramento. Hopefully it will go over the Sierra Nevada mountain range into Nevada and off across the country without stopping.

It is almost four o'clock in the morning and in five hours the three escapees will be noted as missing and one of the biggest manhunts in American history will commence several hours later when it is determined that they are really gone off of the Rock. But not before the east-bound freight train that carries a sleeping Frank Morris is far away from the slowly widening net that will spread out from the San Francisco Bay area trying to ensnare him.

When Frank awakens he discovers to his chagrin that it is getting light and the car is not empty. There is another man about his age lying at the back of the car asleep. Frank moves up to take a closer look and sees that the man is not well. His legs are twitching.

He is burning up with fever and is more in a coma than just asleep. Frank watches him closely but after the train begins moving rapidly from Sacramento to the Sierra Frank dozes fitfully again. As the train starts climbing the grade into the Sierra the man awakens.

"Who the hell are you and why are you in my car?" he asks.

Frank comes quickly to life and responds to the man's question.

"You're in no shape to question me pal, and if it's 'Your car', you shouldn't have left the door open. You never know who's lurking around in neighborhoods like this. Don't worry; I'm not going to harm you. You look like you've already done that for me. You're in bad shape buddy. What's wrong with you?" Frank asks.

The man relaxes a bit and seems to forget about his challenge. "I've got a bad liver. The VA clinic I went to a while back in LA said I was in the last stages of cirrhosis and I had to stop drinking immediately. I wouldn't let them do anything more and skipped town as soon as I could. But they were right; I've kept up my bad habits and it's gotten much worse. Speakin' of bad habits, you don't have a bottle on you, do you? I need a little painkiller. I feel like I'm burning up and my guts are on fire," Frank's traveling mate whispers.

"Sorry pal, they don't allow booze where I just came from. Go back to sleep and I'll keep watch,"

Frank offers and the stranger falls back into a deep but troubled sleep. He doesn't seem to be a threat to anyone anymore. Frank removes his pouch and places it under the man's head. The man sleeps more comfortably. Frank goes back near the door and dozes as well. When he awakens somewhere near the Yuba Gap high in the Sierra, he finds that his boxcar companion is no longer rasping and tossing about. In fact, he isn't moving at all. He is dead.

Frank rolls the body over and finds the man's wallet. There is a driver's license with a few years left on it, a tattered Social Security card, and one folded letter. There are only a few small bills but the ID's represent a new identity for Frank and the clothes, dirty or not, are better than his prison outfit. Frank quickly strips the man to his underwear and don's his pants. The fit isn't too bad but the smell is dreadful. He pulls his rumpled new shirt from its pouch and rolls the tattered prison pants and shirt, and his life vest, and the dead guy's shirt into the pouch to be disposed of later in a manner that will assure that no one will ever find them.

As the train moves along the summit of the Sierra pass, Frank rolls the dead body out of the door and watches it plummet into the steep canyon at the edge of the tracks. Frank figures the creatures out there will make short shrift of the body and he can safely assume the identity of one Christopher Stokes.

The reincarnated Frank Morris jumps off the train in the Nevada hinterland well past Reno and makes his way north burying his prison garb in a fairly deep grave covered with rocks where it will rot in peace.

He makes his way undetected by moving at night and sleeping by day. He uses some of his limited money to buy day-old bread and cheap filling food. He holds back a little money to buy some more presentable clothes and a razor. He steals only enough food to keep up his strength. He hopes that no one notices the small amount of food he pilfers so there are no complaints to the authorities and no trail to follow for anyone looking for him. He travels in stream beds from time-to-time so as to fool any search dogs that may be following him. He saw that trick in an old black-and-white B movie that starred Steve Cochran he thinks.

But that is all a precaution that isn't needed. No one is following him. The authorities find the raft on Angel Island. They come to the convenient conclusion that Morris and the Anglins have been swept out under the bridge into the not so pacific Pacific and are now food for fish.

The authorities still respond to tips but they feel in their hearts that they are all useless and will lead to naught; the three escapees are dead. They don't close the file but move on to other more important matters. (The file will stay open until the last escapee reaches one hundred years of age).

Frank, or Chris as he hopes to be known, is not aware that the FBI is slowly giving up on the search, but for some reason he begins to relax. He is still unceasingly wary and vigilant but he figures time and distance are on his side. The further north he travels the better off he feels about his chances of actually getting all the way free of those he feels must surely be in pursuit. But as he moves inexorably north into wide-open spaces he is beginning to have a sense of unease. He has spent a goodly portion of his adult life in regimented confinement, existing in small highly-controlled spaces. He is becoming uncomfortable in the seemingly endless wilderness he is slowly traveling through. The feeling of unease isn't completely debilitating but it is worrisome and something he has to deal with almost every waking moment. But he is sure the sense of dread will subside and he will be more comfortable with his freedom as the days and nights move on.   He takes a big chance by going into a thrift store in a town along the way. Frank wanders around the store picking out an assortment of clothes. He finds a dented canteen, a pair of khaki pants and shirt, a pair of serviceable boots, some socks, a battered hat, and a tattered rucksack. In the used-book bin he finds a copy of "The Count of Monte Cristo" and adds it to his pile of goods. He places his purchases on the counter in the front of the store. The cashier is an old man in a plaid shirt and overalls.

"Howdy, partner. You just drivin' through?"

"You could say that. Got a job up north," Frank replies.

"That's good. I'll just ring you up and you can be

on your way," the cashier says as he slowly begins writing each item on a sales pad.

There is a black-and-white TV on the wall behind and out of the view of the cashier. Frank sees his own face staring back at him on the TV screen and then watches the rest of the newscast in a state of shock.

"In a new update on the escape from Alcatraz on June 11th FBI agent-in-charge Jack Lapidos comments on a dramatic discovery," the newscaster states as the screen switches to a man in a black suit standing on the shore of Angel Island next to the life raft Frank abandoned the night of the escape.

The FBI agent addresses the camera.

"This is the homemade raft used in the escape. It was found a while back washed up on the shore of Angel Island. Personal papers and effects of the Anglin brothers were found in a waterproof pouch stuck in the bottom of the raft. It is our opinion that the presence of these personal effects still on the raft confirms that the escapees never made it and were drowned. If they had succeeded in reaching Angel Island with the raft they would have not left these items behind. After the most rigorous and exhaustive manhunt in U.S. law- enforcement history there has been no sign of the escapees. There is no other conclusion that can be made other than that Frank Morris, and Clarence and John Anglin are dead."

The TV picture switches back to the announcer in the studio.

"With that it would appear that Alcatraz's no-escape record is still intact. Now to the weather....."

"That sure is something ain't it. I was hoping they made it. How about you?" the cashier asks.

Still in shock all that Frank can think of to say is "I guess."

The cashier comes to the book but doesn't enter it on the sales slip. "I didn't know we had a copy of 'The Count of Monte Christo'. Didn't you read it as a kid?"

"Yeah, but I don't remember much about it. I'm looking forward to reading it again," Frank answers regaining his composure after seeing himself on the TV set.

"All I remember is that there was this prison on an island near a big city and the count escaped from it."

"That sounds vaguely familiar." Frank replies.

"You know, since we both have great taste in reading material I'm throwin' in the book for free" the cashier says as he hands Frank a bag with his purchases. Frank hands him several rumpled bills. As he carefully but quickly heads for the door he hears the cashier's voice yelling at him.

"Hey, wait right there."

Frank slowly turns and faces the cashier.

"You forgot your change."

Two days later when his dread of "open spaces" has subsided to manageable proportions but as he is getting ready to set off on yet another night trek north he has the eerie feeling that he is being watched. He makes a cursory check of the meager undergrowth nearby, chalks it off to nerves, and moves out into the darkening night. But all night as he moves north he has the feeling that he is being followed. He hears a noise behind him. He spins around and could swear he sees movement in the bushes to the left. But the movement is low to the ground; more like an animal than a man. He continues his night's walk but now he is aware that something is definitely following behind him. When he stops, it stops, but after a while when no untoward advancement is made by his hidden walking companion he relaxes. He slows his pace as the dawn rises to his right and looks for a place to bed down for the day. Nothing is heard from his mysterious fellow traveler and when he starts out into the darkening sky in the evening there is no sign of him, her, or it. But later in the night he senses the presence of what he now considers to be if not a friend, a companion. This nocturnal game of tag continues until one evening as he awakens from a dreamless sleep he discovers he is not alone. Calmly sitting about ten yards to his left is what he is sure is a wolf. Over the next few days Frank decides that his new friend can't be a wolf. Wolves travel in packs and are not good companions for humans. And each day his fellow traveler is coming closer and closer. He stops when Frank stops at dawn and starts when Frank starts walking at nightfall. Slowly he comes closer till one day Frank holds out his hand and the dog takes the last step and nuzzles it.

This simple act seems to form a bond between the two that is closer than he has ever had with any living creature.

Chris looks closely at his new friend and quietly talks to him. "I know you're not a wolf. You have to be a dog; maybe a shepherd-mix of some kind. While I assume you have a perfectly good name I'm not privy to what it is. You've got no tags or even a collar. So I'll have to have to give you a new name. It doesn't require much thought. You look like a wolf so 'Wolf' will be your name. I guess we're both sort of lone wolves so let's keep each other company. What do you say, Wolf, you want join up?"

Wolf answers by lying down and placing his head on his paws. Two's company.

One morning as Chris and Wolf are bedding down for the day, Chris remembers his boxcar namesake's letter in what is now *his* wallet. He pulls out the wallet and looks at the envelope. It is from a town somewhere in Utah. The letter is dated years in the past and apparently from old Chris's daughter. She suggests that it is best that he does not return for a visit. She will write when she feels the time is right. He can't decipher the signature. Frank guesses that that time never came. And now it never will. The old Chris is dead. The new Chris is sure not headed for Utah. He tears up the letter and throws the confetti to the wind.

If the old Chris is dead, it is best that the old Frank is dead as well. He wouldn't last more than a couple of months outside of prison. He was a lousy criminal but a great escape artist. And he's just made the escape of the century. Best quit while he's ahead. He will permanently adopt Chris's name and his identity. But he knows becoming a new person will take a long time to really accomplish. A new name is a start. He hopes the rest will follow. He'll have to make it work. There is no other choice. Chris and Wolf, move north.

Somewhere near the Montana border he spots an old green pick-up truck pulled off of the road. As he approaches the truck it seems that it is empty. On the door it says "Feltondale Hardware" in a black and gold script; pretty fancy for an old pick-up. Chris peers through the window and is startled to find an older man lying across the seat fast asleep or maybe even dead. He doesn't seem to be breathing. Chris goes around to the passenger side and opens the door. A closer look reveals that the man is alive but he is surely dead to the world. Chris gently touches his shoulder and begins to quietly shake him. The old man opens his eyes and stares at Chris not really seeming to register where he is.

"Are you alright?" asks Chris.

The old man seems to focus his eyes and begin to get his bearings. "I was feeling dizzy and I pulled over to the side of the road. I remember looking in my shirt pocket for my heart pills and coming up with nothing. I felt too weak; I just had to lie down. I have no idea how long I have been here. Do you know what time it is?"

"I think it's about six P.M.," Chris replies.

"Good Lord, I've been lying here for over an hour. I was headed back to town from the Grimsley ranch where I had delivered a bunch of fencing. I should have never been out here but I wanted to give old Grimsley the best service I could and I don't have any help at the hardware store. I usually have a high-school kid who comes in after school but school's out and he took off with his folks for a vacation before he starts back to work with me full-time for the summer. I got my sister to come in and mind the store while I was gone but she doesn't like working outside of the house so she's probably mad that I disappeared. My name's Dill by the way," the old man rambles as he works his way up to a sitting position. "I still feel a little weak; I must have left my nitro pills back at the store. Sorry, I'm running on, what's your name?"

"My name is Chris Stokes. Glad to meet you. How far ahead is this town you're from?" Chris nods by way of introduction.

"It's only about twelve miles from here but I still don't feel very sharp. If you're headed to Feltondale maybe you could drive this truck for me. I'll show you around my store when we get there and I'll even throw in a free dinner over at Julia's Cafe. What do you say?"

"Sounds good to me. My dog, Wolf, can ride in the bed if that's okay with you. On the way you can tell me about your store, or maybe just take it easy. I haven't driven a truck recently but it will all come back to me I'm sure; like a bicycle," Chris answered.

After a couple of false starts Chris gets the truck moving up the deserted road on the way to his future.

CHAPTER TWO .... July 1962, MONTANA

It is a mild summer's day in southwestern Montana. There's a cloudless sky above the small town of Feltondale that is situated alongside a river that meanders through a large flat valley. In the distance, saw-toothed mountains are a pale-gray purple.

The central east-west thoroughfare of the town is aptly named Main Street. It is Saturday and the four-block-long downtown is busy with people and an almost equal number of dogs.

A glance up and down the side streets reveals the homes of most of the town's residents. The homes to the north are more charming, and in some cases even stately. Most are in better repair, when compared with those to the south of Main Street. There, the homes are smaller and a little rough around the edges and there are a few commercial ventures just south of Main Street as well as several large Victorians that have been converted to apartments. Further to the south, train tracks run parallel to Main Street but they are in disrepair as the trains no longer pass through here. The rest of the citizens who depend on all that the town has to offer live on the numerous ranches that surround it.

There are three churches in Feltondale: two in the more affluent part of town to the north of Main Street, and one on the south side. The first church, in the upper reaches of the town, is the small Episcopal Church which is similar to the many Anglican chapels that dot the English countryside. Several blocks away is the larger but more austere Saint Paul's Lutheran Church. The other Protestants in the area meet where they can. South of Main Street on Taylor is the Catholic Church, Saint Mary's. It comes replete with a rectory and a three-room school. The church had fallen into disrepair but after numerous bake sales, second collections, and rummage sales, the parishioners had collected enough money to repair the roof, paint all of the buildings, and generally spruce up the church grounds. On the first Saturday of the work detail the parishioners were shocked to see an army of volunteers from all over the town coming down the street to lend a hand. They were armed with an assortment of shovels, hoes, ladders and other tools. With all of that man and woman power the job was quickly done and the church turned into its present spotless state. Saint Mary's immaculate appearance halted forever the nickname used by some of its parishioners; Our Lady of Perpetual Dismay.

As for non-believers, they either stay at home or attend impromptu, non-denominational, come-as-you-are services on Sunday at Smiley's Tap Room.

On Main Street there are one and two story buildings built in a pattern mostly determined by

22

their original usage which has, for the most part, been long forgotten. The second stories, which once were living quarters over the stores below, are now predominately offices with only a few appearing to be vacant and none seeming to be derelict. Most of the storefronts have brick façades with tall windows and doors. They are old but in good repair. There is a mixture of retail establishments on the lower floors typical of a small western town in mid-twentieth century America.

On one corner of Main Street and Taylor, the busiest north-south intersection in town, is the locally-owned Rowan Rexall drugstore that has an ice-cream fountain and serves sandwiches for lunch as well. On the corner across Taylor from the drug store is the Feltondale State Bank. To the west of the drugstore is what you would consider to be the heart of the town; three commercial establishments in one very large building. Built in the 1880's, it is one of the oldest and largest structures in the region. Originally, it housed the hotel in the left third of the building and a huge saloon in the rest.

The hotel's layout is pretty much the same as it was when it was built. But it was completely remodeled in 1919 when the entire building was partially reconfigured. Before the reconfiguration, the rest of the building, attached to the hotel by a double door, was the central attraction of the town in the old wild-west days, the Spring Valley Saloon and Steak House. This larger part of the building was more saloon than steak house and included gambling tables and a long bar that ran almost the entire length of the building from front to back on the far-right wall.

The bar had been carried in a sailing ship around the horn in the 1850's. It then had been hauled over the Sierra to a saloon in Virginia City, Nevada during the boomtown days of the Comstock Lode. When the lode petered out, the bar sat derelict in its boarded-up saloon. David Paul Smiley, the founder of the Spring Valley Saloon, discovered the bar as he was coming back to Montana from California and had it shipped to Feltondale at great expense. It became the centerpiece of his newly-built pleasure palace.

In 1933 the saloon was divided into two businesses. Adjacent to the hotel, and still connected by the double door, is the Feltondale Café and Grill. On the far right of the building, next to the café and grill, and separated by a wall that contains yet another connecting door, is what is left of the liquid-end of the old saloon still resplendent with its enormous oak bar. It is now called Smiley's Tap Room, not because its owner is excessively jovial, but because he is a descendant of the original owner and his last name is Smiley. The middle section of the building is in turn divided into two parts, front to back, and houses The Feltondale Café and Grill. In front, with a plate-glass window facing the street is the café part of this double-barreled food emporium. It started out originally as the Feltondale Café but was renamed in the 1940's "Julia's Café" after the infant daughter of the owners, Lee and Kelly Scott. She still runs the café that bears her name written on the front window in red and gold. At the rear of the building behind the cafe is the Feltondale Grill which is only open for lunch and dinner and serves a variety of steaks and a few other up-scale items. It is casually known as "Luke's" after the man who runs it, Julia's older brother. A shared kitchen separates the two eating establishments. A long hall that runs from front to back, gives egress from the street to both the grill in the rear, and a stairway that leads up to the law offices of Felton and Son, Attorneys at Law, that occupy the second story above both the café and grill, and the bar as well.

Elsewhere along Main Street is the office of the Feltondale Gazette, the Rialto movie theater, Jackie's dress shop, Gene's western-wear store, the Barton-Colby variety store, and Hooker's IGA grocery store with a full-service butcher. Ken's Barber Shop doubles as an informal lending library as Ken and his wife Kay are voracious readers who enjoy sharing and discussing the books in their library which is located both in his shop and her beauty salon which is next door. If you want to find out what is going on in the town, state, nation, or world, then these two shops are your best bet for lively discourse and diverse opinions. And, yes, religion and politics are often fair game. Above these two tonsorial establishments are the medical offices of the town. Above the barber shop is the medical office of Doctor Harder and across the hall is where the town dentist Doctor Prawat hangs his shingle. The rest of Main Street is populated by the usual assortment of service shops that even includes an enterprise that is indigenous to the area; Siegfried's House of Taxidermy.

Instead of building a new modern city hall with hard-earned tax-payers money, one of the older two-story brick buildings, one door off of Main Street, was renovated into city offices. There's a chamber for public meetings and several ground-level rooms for the town clerk, the town's deputy sheriff, and room for further expansion.

On the busiest corner in the town, siding on Taylor Street with its front door facing Main, is the architectural gem of downtown; Feltondale Hardware. This cavernous store occupies two retail spaces in adjacent buildings with storage on the floors above. It is a half-a-block deep extending to the alley at the rear. The building is in pristine condition having been lovingly restored by its second-generation owner. On the sidewalk, in front of the store, is a display of gardening implements along with an assortment of Adirondack chairs complete with footstools which were locally made by a rancher in a workshop he set up in one of his unused barns. He sold his ranch and these are the last chairs available for sale.

The green pickup truck pulls into the alley behind the Feltondale Hardware store and Dill and Chris enter the store through the back door. Wolf stays in the pick-up bed.

Dill walks up toward the front of the store. Chris hangs back and slowly takes in the expansive interior. The ceilings are high, at least twelve feet, and made of ribbed wooden slats darkened with age. There is a row of ceiling fans spaced about ten feet apart all the way to the back of the store. They are operating at a lethargic speed that moves little air and barely disturbs the dust. There are straight rows of wooden display shelving stacked to the gunnels with every imaginable manner of hardware, small appliances, tools, and even what appear to be horse shoeing supplies for the local farriers.

Near the main entrance is a large oak counter. Behind the counter's glass front, under lock and key, is a variety of expensive items such as Swiss Army knives, fishing reels, and boxes of ammunition. An older lady, presumably Dill's sister, walks out of the front door and Dill takes her place behind the counter. Chris sees him in a whole new light. He is in his element and looks a lot less vulnerable than he did in the truck. He is a tall, almost gaunt, man with thinning dark hair and glasses. He could be anywhere from fifty to seventy and he seems to be relaxed and completely over whatever was wrong with him in the truck. Chris supposes he got hold of his pills and took one or maybe two. They sure seem to have worked.

"Hey Chris, come on up here," Dill calls out.

27

As Chris approaches the long wooden counter with the ancient brass cash register, Dill smiles at him.

"So now I'm feeling my old self back here in my usual place behind the counter. What do you think? Did you get a chance to look around? It's a big place and I'm not only the owner but I'm the chief cook and bottle washer as well. My full name's Dillard Staunton. We haven't really formally met," Dill states as he extends his hand.

"I'm Chris Stokes, Dill, pleased to meet you." Chris shakes his hand with a firm grip. "How can you run this place all by yourself? It looks like you need some serious help here."

"If we had come through the front door you would have seen a 'Help Wanted' sign there. But it's been gathering dust. The older folks around here all have jobs, and the younger ones just want to get out of town as soon as they can. So it's been tough for me," Dill explains. "I've run this place pretty much by myself. My daughter Penny used to give me a hand but she went off to college and now lives in New York City working for a big-time publisher on Madison Avenue. She was sort of my right-hand and I can tell you I feel her absence every day in more ways than one. As I mentioned in the truck, I have a local kid, William, who comes in after high school during the week for a couple of hours but other than that it's just me. And I'm no spring chicken. I've been gradually slowing down over the years and it gets harder and harder to cover all the bases here," Dill pauses. "Say, you wouldn't be interested in a job would you Chris? You sure saved my bacon out there on the road and you seem like a trustworthy fellow."

Chris takes only a few seconds to reply. "A job is just what I'm looking for. What does your job entail? I'm interested."

"Well I guess the job I'm offering is for someone to become my new right-hand. I need someone to learn the business from the bottom up and inside out; someone who is in it for the long haul. You'd start by taking the delivered merchandise from the loading dock at the back of the store in the alley, and stocking the shelves down here or stowing the goods upstairs for the future. Once you learn that part, there are customers to be waited on, bookwork to be done, and this cash register to be run. The ideal person for this job would have at least a nodding acquaintance with all kinds of skills from carpentry to plumbing. The job requires a lot of different skills and would take a man not only of many talents and aptitudes, but one with an ability to quickly learn new ones. I know that's a tall order, but how do you see yourself fitting into that description?" Dill finishes.

After a long pause, Chris looks up from staring at his hands and responds. "Well, I fit the bill in some ways. I have experience working with the public as a librarian, though I could improve my people skills. I've worked as a bookkeeper as well for a short while. I have experience working as a carpenter in several furniture shops and I've done a bit of painting. I have a good knowledge of most wood-working tools. I've had training in electrical work and I'm pretty savvy about that entire field. I've done a little welding and soldering work but I don't know much about plumbing. But you could say I'm a quick study and I could pick up whatever it is that you think I should know without too much trouble. To tell you the truth, this job seems perfect to me. I've worked a lot of odd jobs in my life and I'm looking to start over. I don't mind starting at the bottom as long as there's a future and there's room to learn and grow," Chris replies.

"I say, that's quite a resume you've got there Chris. Do you have any references?" Dill asks.

"Up to now I've never stayed in one place long enough to earn a reference though I did work in one furniture shop a while longer than most of my jobs. I never got a reference though. I guess I wasn't looking that far ahead. I do have a driver's license and a Social Security card however," and with that Chris pulls out a thin, well-worn billfold and produces both items for Dill's inspection.

After perusing both the license and the Social Security card for what seems to be an eternity, Dill appears to be gathering his thoughts. But before he can speak, the bell on the front door rings and a customer walks up to the counter. Not wanting to be in the way, Chris backs away and continues his inspection of the mountains of merchandise on display. When the customer finally leaves Chris returns to the counter.

"I'm glad that customer interrupted our conversation Chris," Dill states as he hands back Chris's identification. "It gave me a chance to think over this whole situation. I've had that sign in the window for a long time. I guess I was looking for someone to walk in here with all the qualifications for the job and years of experience. But we don't have many folks moving into town; mostly it's the other way around. And as I said, I should have known that nobody local here would be of any use. And then you come along. You don't seem the kind that would take off at the slightest provocation. And somehow it seems to me that maybe you've seen all the bright lights you can handle. Maybe it's time I got off my duff and made a decision. That sign in the window isn't getting any younger and neither am I. Could be you're the kind of guy I've been looking for and I just didn't know it," Dill pauses for several contemplative moments and continues. "You know Chris, I think I have an answer for both of us; how about I start you out on probation of some sort? If, at the end of a month we both like what we see, we can think of something more permanent and lay out a course for you to follow in your job here. It looks like we could use each other. What do you say to that Chris?" Dill asks.

A slow smile crosses Chris's face and he shakes Dill's hand. "You've got yourself an understudy Dill. Let's try it out. I have no doubt it's what I've been looking for and I hope in a month you'll feel the same way. When do I start?"

"Right away, but there's one more thing I think we need to add to the mix to make things run smooth. This is a small town. And small towns don't cotton to strangers. That sort of insular behavior could make our lives miserable but I think I have a way to solve this dilemma if it's all right with you. Let me offer a solution on how you can fit in here quicker and with a minimum of fuss. What if we were related? That would answer a lot of questions folks would have before they even have them. My father's older brother married late in life and had a daughter name of Abigail. She went by the name of Gabby, and she was always headstrong and fought with her parents before she was old enough to talk. She was a wild one. She up and left town on her seventeenth birthday never to be heard of again. She was an only child and her folks never got over her desertion. They didn't live long after that. So, why don't we embellish on that story a bit. There's no one left to contradict us except my sister and she'll go along with the story if I ask her to. What if Gabby went out to Utah and got married a guy name of Stokes and had a kid; namely you? That way you'd be my cousin and the folks in town here would be more prone to accept you at face value. That sound like a good plan Chris?"

"You're the boss Dill. I don't have any living relations so you'd be my only my family. Let's say I heard about you from my Mom when I was a kid and all these years later I looked you up on a whim," Chris says with a smile.

Dill returns the smile and reaches into the cash register. "Welcome to the family Chris. I'll introduce you to your aunt when she gets used to the idea of your existence. Here's a few bucks advance. I'll take it out of your first paycheck next week. You look like you could use a haircut and maybe you need a few other items. If you don't have a place to stay yet, there's a boarding house one block south of Main Street on Elm. Mrs. Buffington, who for some strange reason likes to be called Aunt Imelda, will take care of you. She's got a small yard out in back and I'm sure she'd welcome your dog as well. Just tell her I sent you. So that's it then. I'll see you in the morning; eight o'clock sharp."

CHAPTER THREE ... June 1962, THE PACIFIC

The *Stella del Sud* has seen better days; perhaps better decades. She has a dull-red hull and black sides. Both are liberally sprinkled with patches of rust. There is little rust on her topsides because they are easier to reach and they are painted in various shades of gray. In a storm she would almost disappear. Her freeboard is covered with many layers of dull-black paint that try to conceal years of bumping into piers, rubbing against docks, and fending off the flotsam and jetsam she has encountered on the high seas. She seems sea-worthy, if well-worn and dated. She'll probably out live her usefulness before she falls into terminal disrepair. The old gal has more than a few good years left in her.

She was built in 1938 and survived World War II and the 1950's. But the increasing use of container ships is putting a dent in her ability to scrounge cargos to carry.

Most of the tramp steamers owned by the large shipping companies "went East" having been sold to Asian shipping companies. The *Stella del Sud* was not so lucky. She was sold to a small Italian shipping firm headquartered on the Adriatic. She was one of two tramps they bought and sent to the Pacific to ply their trade.

She is under the almost autonomous control of her
Greek-American Captain Dmitri Poppolus. As long as
he sends the owners close to what their share should
be on each cargo he carries, and as long as he sends a
somewhat accurate record of his expenses for crew,
fuel, and repairs, they let him be. There is really no
way they can control him anyway so why not take
what they can and be content with the pickings. As
for the Captain, he is as happy as the proverbial clam.
It is almost as if he were Master as well as Captain.

Captain Dmitri is perched on his captain's chair on
the bridge of the *Stella* looking out at the calm sea
ahead of them. If he were standing, it would be
immediately apparent that he is a short and sturdy
man; stocky and slightly overweight. He has a
swarthy complexion typical of a man from the
Mediterranean. He always looks like he is in need of a
shave no matter how often he drags a razor across his
face, and he sports a large, bushy, black, walrus-type
mustache that is his most well-cared for facial feature.

He is dressed in his usual outfit: a black uniform of
sorts made of heavy twill; more sturdy than
fashionable. The trousers are held up by the
combination of a wide black-leather belt around his
burgeoning girth and a pair of black braces. The
uniform jacket is double breasted and in much need of
the attention of a dry cleaner. It sports a row of bright
gold buttons that are incongruously well polished.
They have an anchor motif in keeping with the
occupation of their owner. His jacket is usually open

and reveals an expanse of clean but rumpled white broad cloth. When the Captain moves about, the butt of a 45 caliber Army-issue automatic ensconced in a black-leather shoulder holster is occasionally, and purposely, visible. As far as he knows, it is the only gun aboard the vessel. No one knows whether it is loaded; nor do they want to. Captain Bligh might not have ended up in a row boat if he had had one of these. To top off the Captain's nautical ensemble is a modified Greek sailor's cap with an unpolished leather bill. It has no insignia of rank on either the cap itself, or on the bill. Its only adornment is a band of black-braid embroidery around the bottom. It has seen better days but adds a bit of height and authority to the Captain and he is rarely seen without it, indoors or out.

There is not a cloud on the horizon and the barometer mercury is steady. The seas are calm with a light breeze coming across the starboard quarter of the bow. The Captain is well pleased with himself. He has completely provisioned his ship with fuel and food in Hawaii and is now making a steady eight knots toward his next port of call in Fiji. From there it's on to Indonesia where he has to deliver the diesel generators he picked up in San Francisco. He vividly remembers just what happened there to bring him to his present state of serenity. He closes his eyes and it is as if he were almost there.

The *Stella* is in the most costly port on the west coast and his fortunes are beginning to take a rollercoaster ride. Luckily, he had no problem with the notorious Harry Bridges and his lead-legged, sticky-fingered, San Francisco stevedores. They had loaded the four generators into the forward hold using the ship's forward cargo derricks with a minimum of effort. But it cost like hell.

At eight PM, the Captain's fortunes take a downturn when he is told by the First Mate that their two cooks have not returned to the ship. He has until midnight before he has to pay another day's dock fees so they wait. By 11:45 PM the rascals have not shown their faces. He figures they have gotten tired of all the complaints about their horrible cooking and have resigned from the ship's complement without as much as a goodbye. There is no more waiting. They untie from the pier and set sail for Hawaii without any cooks on board. Thank God for peanut butter and sardines; two stalwart staples that are always in great supply in the larder.

He figures he'll have to "volunteer" two of the ordinary seamen on board to be cooks. If anybody complains he can invoke the "Moose-Turd Pie" rule he heard about from an American ship's chandler in San Pedro a long time ago. It seems that the workers on the transcontinental railroad in America had a unique system of selecting cooks as there were no cooks hired by the railroad to man the cook car. One of the railroad workers was selected by the job boss to be cook. It was a thankless job and nobody wanted the long hours, the short pay, and all the complaints. So, as the story goes, if anyone bitched about the food, he then became the cook.

One day the current cook was walking around the outside of the cook car when he spotted a gigantic steaming moose turd. A grin slowly came to his face. At last he had a way to get out of the cook's job once and for all. He scooped the turd up on the business end of a flat shovel, took it to the cook car, and started to work.

He first created a large fluffy pie shell and placed the moose turd gently in it with some salt and pepper. He then placed a lattice crust over the top, brushed it with a mixture of milk and butter, sprinkled it with some parsley flakes, and baked it for forty-five minutes. Then he waited for the work gang to come to the cook car for dinner. He was sure that this would be his last day in this horrible job. Tomorrow he would be out gandy dancing with the regular workers.

When the workers had quit for the day and were all seated awaiting their dinner, he proudly placed the steaming pie in the center of the table and sliced each man a large piece. The men looked at, and smelled, the dish before them with some trepidation. Finally, one of them fitfully placed a forkful in his mouth. After a moment he looked rather ill and spit the mouthful back onto his plate.

"Good grief, that tastes like moose-turd pie!" he yelled and suddenly realizing what he had brought down upon himself he further commented, *"It's good though."*

"Dear God; if it were only that easy," the Captain thinks. "Oh well, we'll do the best we can. We'll just have to put up with the constant complaints of the crew about the god-awful meals. The real problem is that losing two men on his already skeletal crew could be dicey because the cooks filled in on other jobs as well."

Then, when everything looks the bleakest, the Gods intervene; from Olympus or Heaven it really doesn't matter to him. He has adopted a somewhat workable and flexible religion by combining the compassion and peaceful posture of the Christian church, especially Mary, with the powerful lusty gods of ancient Greece. When you're facing treacherous gale-force winds and fifteen-foot waves breaking over your bow, you don't call for help from the likes of Jesus or the Holy Ghost. This is no time to turn the other cheek. All you would get is a wet ass. In this situation what you really need are the old gods, especially Poseidon. He rules the oceans and is powerful enough to calm the raging seas and generally kick some butt.

As the Captain watches the Farallon Islands glide by to the starboard, he finally feels he has left San Francisco behind. The nearest land is something like twenty-seven miles to the stern.

It is then that the Gods smile down upon the stalwart Captain and his trusty old ship. The First Mate, Mike Dolan, enters the bridge with two sorry looking blokes in tow. Mike is a tall and gangly man, all sinew and angles, as if he were a seaborne version of Ichabod Crane. He is dressed in an elongated version of the Captain's uniform but without the shiny brass buttons and the hat. He has big hands, long arms and legs, and a wiry strength; a useful attribute when dealing with a rowdy crew. He is Mutt to the Captain's Jeff.

The two men he has in his grasp are almost as big as Dolan. However, they are much the worse for wear looking as if they'd been keel hauled and left to die on the deck.

"Look what I found stowed away in the forward paint locker Captain," Dolan says as he sits the two of them down on the long bench that lines the port side of the bridge. The Captain takes a closer look. They are big, raw-boned men, somewhere about forty. They both have sheepish grins on their face as if they'd been caught with their hands in the cookie jar. Their clothes are in tatters and they smell decidedly of paint.

But to the Captain they are a sight for sore eyes; a gift from God; any God. They might be two of the men the Coast Guard had called about; but who cares. They are flesh and blood, look to be in good health if somewhat bedraggled, and it seems as if they don't have lot of prospects other than staying right here on

40

the *Stella*. It should be a piece of cake persuading them to join his crew.

First he has to see if they have any nautical experience. Or, even better, maybe they can boil water and make sandwiches.

"Do either of you know anything about the sea and ships?" he asks. Not even waiting for an answer the Captain continues. "Well, I'll give you a brief maritime lesson. Be patient. I'll make this as simple as possible. But I want you to know how things stand.

We are on the good ship *Stella del Sud*, Italian for *The Star of the South*. She is a Three Island tramp steamer built in 1938 in Great Britain by Doxford and Sons. Three Island means she has three built-up parts; one in the bow, this bridge tower right here amidships, and another in the stern; the back to you," the Capitan begins his nautical lecture. "As to the name tramp steamer; well she's a tramp alright but not really a steamer anymore. She was an oil-fired steamer unlike most of the tramp steamers built in the 1930's. She has been refitted with diesel engines. She has always run on oil not coal. It's cheaper and more efficient. But most important to us, we salt-water drifters, is that the *Stella* can be refueled in almost any port in the world," he tells the two brothers as they sit forward in their seats in rapt attention trying to understand what the Captain is trying to explain to them; and not really getting much of it at all.

"As to the word tramp," the Captain   continues,

"while it may describe her current sorry condition most aptly, that's not really what it means. Hell, there have been brand-new ships that were tramps.

Tramp steamers are called that because they have no set itinerary. With no schedule, they sort of 'tramp' around the seven seas. They travel to and from any ports where they can pick up or deliver cargo. They are the vagabonds of the oceans. So, 'tramp' yes; 'steamer' no.

Now, let me tell you about the crew that runs this fine tramp ship. They're a rag-tag bunch from many different races, nationalities, and backgrounds. But they have one common thread that binds them together. They are not fit to do much else than this, or are, for whatever reason, not welcome to reside anywhere else in the civilized world; or both. You'll find a wide assortment of the finest rascals, misfits, and scoundrels the world has to offer on board a ship like this. There are stowaways like you, smugglers, drug addicts, simpletons, union organizers, loan sharks, gamblers, drunks, perverts, preachers, and thieves. And those are just the good guys.

So, we have no other choice than to create our own little world here on board, with our own set of nautical rules to live by. If the rules are obeyed, we all get along and hopefully succeed in our adventurous ventures. If they are not, then the source of conflict is removed. It's that simple. Keep your nose clean and don't look for trouble because you will surely find it if you do. So, enough about us, what do you have to say for yourselves? Let's start with your names. And remember you address me as Captain. Them's the rules."

There is a long pause as if the two men are trying to gather their thoughts and can't seem to find them. One of them finally pipes up.

"Well Captain, we're brothers. I'm John and he's Charles," he pauses as if in thought. "Our last name is Daniels like the sippin' whiskey; no relation though," the youngest-appearing of the two reveals as he grins at the Captain. He then clams up again.

"Well what about some more tidbits about yourselves. I won't ask why or how you got on our ship. You're here. That's all that matters. But where do you hail from? You sound like you are from deep in the American South. Am I right? Enlighten us a little more if you please," the Captain asks as he leans back in his chair as if expecting a revelation.

"Well, we're originally from Georgia. You got that right. Back up in the hills. A place you never heard of; and wouldn't want to. Mom and Dad had fourteen children; seven of each kind," Charlie answers this time.

"And your culinary experience, cooking, anything at all like that in your sordid background? You must have boiled some grits at one time or another, haven't you?" the Captain asks.

"I don't know about that culinary business, Captain, but we can damn sure cook up a storm. We were raised on a small farm out in backwoods Georgia

43

and we lived real close to the land. We all helped out in the kitchen. We raised and slaughtered hogs too. We'd butcher and smoke 'em. Made the best maple-sugar cured hams and bacon you can hope to eat. We've killed and dressed chickens, 'though I never did quite understand what that meant. After all, when you take off all their feathers they're sort of undressed, ain't they. Anyway, our mom made the best fried chicken in a county well known for its fried chicken. And biscuits, my God, you had to cover 'em with gallons of heavy gravy just so they wouldn't float away. So you could say we know our way around a kitchen. And we've done some short order cooking in our time too; slingin' hash and fryin' up all sorts of eggs, and taters, and flapjacks and the like," John answers this time.

"Well that is just what these tired old ears were looking to hear," says the Captain. "We're a good ship of sorts but we could be better by a long shot. That's where you two come in; what all this cooking stuff is about."

"First, let me tell you where you stand," the Captain begins his lecturing again. "Normally stowaways are treated harshly; as if they are no better than slaves. Sometimes they're locked up in the brig but in our case, we use every hand we can get. Stowaways could be considered criminals of a sort. They are generally turned over to the authorities at the next port and hopefully for the Captain, there's a reward on their head which makes it worthwhile.

However, in your case we may be able to work something out. You scratch my back and I'll scratch yours. From the looks of you there is no reason why you would want to return to the states anytime soon. But we may have some use for you right here on the *Stella*," the Captain says as he jumps down from his captain's chair and paces up and down in front of the brothers like a college professor addressing his students.

"Usually when new inexperienced hands join a ship they start at the bottom as ordinary seamen. They do a variety of chores like standing watch, maintaining the equipment on board like the lifeboats, anchors, and the cargo-handling gear. They handle the lines when we dock and leave port. The rest of the time, they perform routine chores such as repairing lines, chipping rust, and painting; always painting. Paint is the glue that holds an old ship like this together.

Here's where you get lucky. If you throw in your lot with this complement of fine ruffians and louts, then you can start one rung up the ladder. You can bypass all that chipping and painting and become the ship's cooks. With your experience you should fit right in. At least we'll give you a try. If you don't succeed, then there are always the cops or the sharks. It looks to me that you don't have a lot of options. We are offering you a home and a job with no questions asked. Your past will be just that; past. The *Stella* is a safe place to escape from the world at large, and your future is as rosy as you want to make it. All you have to do is cook; and as a bonus you'll be paid. We'll start you out with ordinary seaman's wages and if you prove that you can handle the job and I don't hear a lot of complaints from the crew about the grub, then we'll raise your wages to that of able-bodied seamen at some time in the future. That's the deal. Stay aboard, mind the rules, and run the galley. That's the nautical term for a kitchen. By all means, take a minute to think about it," the Captain suggests all the while staring intensely at the two men as if he were trying to hypnotize them into giving the right answer. After a few nods back and forth Charles replies.

"I'd say it's your lucky day Captain, and ours too I guess. You've found yourself two cooks for this old tramp. All we'll need is time to get familiar with your kitchen or galley, and how you store the food and such, and we'll be ready to go."

The Captain produces an audible sigh of relief. Problems solved. Fortunes on the rise.

"Fine lads. We have a larder and stores mate name of Manuel but we call him Manny. He's from the Philippines and he'll show you the ropes. He'll be your right hand man so treat him just that; right. We'll get us a full larder of provisions when we are in Hawaii. Till then you'll have to make do.

Mister Dolan the First Mate, and 'Sir' to you, will see that you get proper clothes, and such, and you can have the bunks of our dear departed shipmates who left us in the lurch that you are going to fill.

All righty then, hop to it and I hope to see a marked improvement in our vittles. By-the-by, we'll even try to commandeer a live little pig in the Islands. We'll see if you can turn pig to passable pork like you said you could. It's not as fancy as changing water into wine, but it will surely do," the Captain finishes his speech making and hops back up onto his captain's chair.

With that, the brothers Daniels find a new floating home and the good ship *Stella del Sud*'s motley crew is going to be well fed; at least after the boys get acquainted with the galley and they pick up more provisions in Hawaii. Till then the brothers will have to make do with peanut butter, sardines and whatever else they can find in the galley.

CHAPTER FOUR ... 1921–1953, MONTANA

If a town ever had a perfectly suited candidate for leading citizen it would be Wesley Felton III. He is a third-generation resident of Feltondale, Montana, and the grandson of the town's namesake.

Wes's grandfather was born in 1856 in Quincy, Massachusetts, "Birthplace of the American Dream", and attended law school at Yale. He moved from the East Coast to the western territories in 1878 and established his law offices on the block-long Main Street in Spring Valley Junction above the fledgling town's most vibrant saloon. (The two other saloons in town were not on Main Street and had much more bawdy and profitable businesses located above them.)

Grandfather Felton knitted together a somewhat loose confederation of residents in and around Spring Valley Junction and was instrumental in incorporating them into a legal town in 1880. He was the town's first mayor and the town was renamed Feltondale in his honor. He married a local girl and Wesley II (never Junior) was born in 1881. His mother never liked the idea of her husband and her son having the same name and she hated the use of "Junior" so she called her son Nate after his middle name; Nathaniel. The name stuck. After the turn of the century Nate too attended and graduated from Yale Law and joined his father in the family law business in the same office above the saloon and became the first "and Son".

By then, the saloon had evolved into a more genteel restaurant and bar. It was still connected to the town's only hotel. Nate brought back a bride from the East Coast and Wes III was born in 1921 seven years before his grandfather died. Wes III's mother was an aloof, haughty, and vacuous woman who never adapted well to the life of a western wife. There was little for a former fledgling society maven to do in Feltondale except to play bridge and lord over the markedly thin, half-baked upper crust of the town.

Wes III was called Wes Trey, or just Trey, until his grandfather died at which time he reverted to being called just Wes with no III after it. He was proud of his heritage but he felt more comfortable without the numerical suffix tacked onto his name.

Wes's life was pretty much what you would have expected for the scion of such a prestigious family. Like his father and grandfather before him he was the proverbial big frog in a little pond. He was an active, inquisitive child who loved the outdoors. He excelled at high-school sports, especially football, and was a good, if not mercurial, student. But it was his legacy status, not his grades, that got him into Yale following in the footsteps of his father and grandfather. He was destined to become the second "and Son" on the law-office shingle.

In his sophomore year at Yale, World War II broke out and Wes went into the Navy as a junior officer. In 1943 he was assigned to the aircraft carrier *USS Bunker Hill* and served in the Pacific as the American forces hopped from island to island in an inexorable but bloody march north toward Japan.

In May of 1945 the *USS Bunker Hill* was engaged in supporting the invasion of Okinawa in the final months of the war. The land of the rising sun was finally setting. The crew was at their battle stations fending off the kamikaze suicide planes that the Japanese were employing in a last ditch effort to stop, or at least severely impede, the invasion of their homeland.

Wes was running across the flight deck toward the carrier's "island" superstructure when he saw a Zero emerge from the low cloud cover and penetrate the punishing protective ring of fire put up by the *Bunker Hill's* anti-aircraft guns. The suicide pilot was heading straight for the ship. As the Zero reached the ship's flight deck it launched its lethal 500-pound bomb. But while the bomb hit and penetrated the flight deck it failed to explode and exited from the side of the ship doing only minimal damage. It exploded harmlessly as it crashed into the ocean.

The plane itself was another matter. It deliberately crashed into the flight deck destroying many parked warplanes. The remains of the Zero went over the side and into the ocean leaving behind a scene of carnage on the flight deck as the warplanes exploded. The flat top was ablaze with huge fires that shot smoke and flames skyward with the repeated explosions of ammunition and fuel.

Wes was knocked to the deck by the force of the explosions. He was slowly managing to rise when another Zero got through the deadly fire of the antiaircraft guns and plunged into its suicide dive. It dropped its 500-pound bomb and then flew into the flight deck near the superstructure that was the control center; the vital heart of the carrier. This was the prime target of all kamikaze pilots and fortunately for the ship, the Zero just missed hitting the superstructure itself and crashed beneath it. Both the bomb and the remains of the Zero ignited huge gasoline fires and sent more columns of flame and smoke into the sky in an inferno that would surely send the ship and its crew to the bottom if it were not quickly contained.

After the second plane hit, Wes quickly assessed the damage and scrambled to take charge of his designated fire-suppression team. The sailors of the *Bunker Hill* valiantly fought the explosions and fires at a further cost of life, finally putting them out. Wes ran into the flames on numerous occasions to pull out wounded and dead sailors from the twisted wreckage of what was left of the flight deck.

During one rescue attempt Wes was wounded as a piece of shrapnel from an exploding plane lodged in his thigh. While the whole world was exploding around him and he was in the thick of it, he had no thoughts at all that he can remember. It was as if he were numb. He was just reacting to the terror going on around him and doing his duty instinctively.

Three hundred and forty-six sailors and airmen died when the *Bunker Hill* was attacked that day, with forty-three more missing, and two hundred and sixty-four wounded. A part of Wes died alongside his shipmates.

After the smoke and fires had cleared he helped transfer the seriously-wounded men to the *USS Wilkes Barre* which had come alongside the smoldering hulk of the stricken carrier. Wes finally received first aid for his wound and it was determined that he was fit enough to remain with the ship as there was a desperate need for officers on board for the long trip to Hawaii; if they could make it. With the fires finally under control a further assessment was made and it was feared that the *Bunker Hill* was so severely damaged that it could sink if they didn't do some on-the-spot repairs before they began their long journey. The most necessary repairs were miraculously accomplished and the jury-rigged ship finally got under way limping toward Oahu. The trip was slow and tortuous but the *Bunker Hill* finally reached Pearl Harbor.

She was made more seaworthy and readied for a voyage that would finally take her home to the States; well out of harm's way. After receiving outpatient treatment in Hawaii, Wes was able to continue with his ship as she made her way to Bremerton, Washington for extensive repairs.

She was still in dry dock when World War II ended. After a thorough check-up it was determined that Wes's wound had healed enough for him to leave the Navy. He resigned his commission and returned home.

Though Wes considered he was merely doing his duty during the kamikaze attacks, his superiors thought otherwise and he received the Bronze Star for valor and a Purple Heart for his wound. They now reside in his cuff link box.

Wes suffered for months with recurring nightmares of the attacks. After a while they subsided but the attack on the *Bunker Hill* and the ensuing aftermath of horror and carnage remained with him for the rest of his life.

When Wes finally reached home after the war he was rested, and fully recuperated from his wounds. He helped out in the office until the fall when he returned to Yale and finished the undergraduate degree that the war had interrupted. Upon graduation, he immediately entered Yale Law as was preordained by family tradition and received his law degree in 1951.

It wasn't until he had returned home from Yale and took his place next to his father for a while in the family practice as the second "and Son" that the uneasiness began. Like a lot of World War II veterans, Wes was not satisfied with just coming back home and starting up where he had left off. His horizons had been expanded. His life in the confines of Feltondale was not enough of what he wanted; at least not yet. He'd done everything that was required of him by his family, tradition, and even what he expected from himself. His life had been laid out for him and he had accepted that with no objections. Maybe it was a case of "watch out for what you wish for; you might just get it". He got it all right.

His schooling was complete and he had settled into the routine at the law office for three years. He liked practicing law. He dealt with all sorts of legal problems from simple wills to complex disputes involving the riparian rights of various ranches in the vicinity. It was all right, but there had to be more. He had seen some of the world, all-be-it from the flight deck of an aircraft carrier.

Perhaps, he thinks, he should take a year or so off and travel some more before he loses all chance of breaking free. Maybe he'll find more direction and contentment in his life. It is as if he knows he eventually belongs in Feltondale, but isn't sure why.

And if he takes some time off he is confident that he will be a better asset to the town that bears his name and that he knows he loves. Hopefully he will be more engaged and focused when he returns.

His father isn't happy about the idea. He doesn't understand how Wes feels, but he has never been the adventurous sort. Wes's mom doesn't seem to mind, but there again she never has minded much about anything. So Wes decides for himself. He packs his suitcase and leaves for Europe.

They say you can't go home again. In Wes Felton's case, he does make it back home; but it takes him quite a while. It will be eight years before he returns for good, but he comes back a more mature and experienced man ready to settle down and devote his efforts to making Feltondale a better place to live. He hopes he can help to improve the economic prospects of his hometown.

It is a worthy goal. The matured man just may be able to achieve it.

CHAPTER FIVE ... 1931-1955, MONTANA

Penny Staunton almost wasn't born. There were serious complications at her birth that threatened both her and her mother. She survived. Her mother did not.

Her father, Dillard, or "Dill" as he is more commonly known is a second generation citizen of Feltondale. His father founded Feltondale Hardware shortly after the town was formed in 1882. Dill succeeded in the family business in 1918 when his father died of the influenza.

Penny was born April of 1931. She was adored from the minute of her birth. Perhaps this is because she is a daily reminder of the brief joy her father had known during his short and tragic marriage to her mother, Nicole.

From the moment her father held Penny in his arms at the hospital, he knew that he would dedicate his life to raising her. Dill's sister Martha lives with him in the family house and helped to raise Penny. Without Martha, his task would have been impossible. And Penny adores her. It was almost as if she were Penny's mother; a position Martha is happy to embrace.

When Penny was barely tall enough to peek over the counter she helped her father at the hardware store. She learned how to run the business over the years as if by osmosis. She was both her father's right-hand man, and the apple of his eye. In short, she was as bright as a new Penny.

Penny was a shy young girl, especially around people her own age. In spite of that, or perhaps because of it, she excelled at school, enjoying books more than people. This love of academics paid off and Penny was at the top of her class and the valedictorian of her high-school graduation.

But her success is a mixed blessing. Her academic prowess has not gone unnoticed and her English teacher, who is also her career counselor, is impressed with her writing skills and becomes her mentor. Under Mrs. Paulson's tutelage she is encouraged to apply for a college scholarship and two months before she graduates she is offered a full scholarship to attend a small, private, liberal-arts college in the state capitol. Her father is both thrilled and devastated. Although he and Martha will miss her terribly, both at home and at the hardware store, he has no choice but to encourage her to go.

Her father and Martha are bursting with pride as they sit in the front row on the lawn of Feltondale High School on a warm day in May and watch her graduate.

Penny leaves for college in early September of 1949, still somewhat shy but eager to embrace the chance she has earned to further her education and learn something of the world outside Feltondale and the hardware store.

At college she soars. Each day is a joy to her and she succeeds beyond her and Mrs. Paulson's wildest dreams.

While she is a great success in her academic endeavors, her private life is less than stellar. She is still a bit shy and considers boys her own age to be somewhat juvenile and generally uninteresting; which, due to her years of living in a world dominated by adults, they are. It is nothing new; boys her own age have never impressed her.

But this leads to trouble for her in her senior year. Unbeknownst to her father, whom she sees only during the holidays and the summer break, she has become involved with a not-so-young English Lit professor who bestows upon her a liberal introduction in the ways of the world.

But the affair does not go well. He leaves her momentarily broken hearted when he severs their relationship. He is afraid that a long-term liaison will stand a good chance of being discovered, and will jeopardize his freshly won tenure at the college.

Penny recovers from the affair and returns home at the end of her college days with not only a bachelor's degree with honors but a slight, self-imposed, feeling of shame, or maybe just disappointment, that she has allowed her character to be so easily besmirched; and by such a cowardly lothario.

Her father is delighted to have her back; both at home and at the store. They fall back into the easy relationship they had enjoyed before she went off to school.

Several contented years pass before Penny begins to feel stifled. She has a few friends her age in town but it seems that life is going to pass her by if she doesn't do something to put her hard-earned college degree to better use. Her college counselor, Miss McCutcheon, had suggested that she would do well in the publishing business and had several contacts at publishing houses in New York. Though the prospect intrigued her at the time, Penny had not been tempted, knowing that she would return to Feltondale and her father when she graduated.

But after two years, she is not so sure that she made the right choice. She writes a letter to Miss McCutcheon and asks if she would still be able to recommend her to her New York contacts.

After what seems to be an eternity, Penny receives a life-changing letter in return. Indeed, Miss McCutcheon's good friend at Guild Publishing, on Madison Avenue at 53rd Street in Manhattan, was impressed by Penny's college resume and writes that she would like to meet with her if she would be interested in securing a position as a fledgling assistant in the editorial department at their firm. Next to the mailroom, this is the bottom rung in the publishing world. Could Penny travel to New York for an interview?

Penny is thrilled at the chance to broaden her horizons and put her college successes to work. Once again her father is faced with a separation from his daughter. As before, he puts Penny's future above his need to have her at his side, and in April of 1955 he drives her to the capital where she boards a train for New York.

CHAPTER SIX ... 1962, MONTANA

There was never a doubt in Chris's mind that he would pass the probation period at the hardware store with flying colors. That is unless something from outside the world of Feltondale interferes with the process. But so far it hasn't.

Chris has a strong work ethic when he is motivated and, as he promised Dill, he is a fast learner.

And now he is enjoying the fruits of his labor. Dill has assured him that he has earned a permanent position, if he wants it. And he has assured Dill that he does. For one of the few times in his life he feels like he is on the right path and that he has the wherewithal to stay on it. He's come a long way in the short time that has passed since he drove Dill into town on that summer day.

With four week's pay in his pocket he feels he can look to the future with neither ambivalence nor dread. First on his agenda is finding another place to live. It doesn't have to be fancy but it needs to be quiet. His work involves dealing with the public most of the day and he'd rather limit that in his off time. The boarding house has been a fine place to live as a stop-gap measure but Chris has never been a fan of communal dining no matter how good the food is. He likes to read while he eats, not talk. What Chris craves is not necessarily solitude, but a little peace and quiet would be nice.

So he begins to look for a place to live where he can be on his own. He has enough money left over after paying Dill back the amount he had advanced him. He can afford the up-front costs of a deposit and the first month's rent but not much more. So he religiously scours the few want ads in the paper and checks the bulletin board at the Laundromat every day.

He finally finds a small apartment on the south side of Main Street. Not the more sedate section of town north of Main, but what his finances dictate is feasible at the moment. There will always be a chance to move up if and when he feels the need.

The apartment is above a two-car garage that is used for storage by the farm-equipment repair shop next door. The garage has little activity and the repair shop is open the same hours as the hardware store, so there is little chance it will interfere with Chris's solitude. There is a large fenced side yard that should serve as place for Wolf during the day.

His new home is very modest: one bedroom, a large bath, a living room with corner windows that look down the street toward the railroad right-of-way, and a small kitchen that is quite suitable to a man whose most complicated meal is toast and coffee. The place is decorated in early anything. The furnishings are eclectic, and not in the good sense of the word.

There is a colonial maple couch with green plaid cushions in the living room, a gray Formica table in the kitchen, and a knotty-pine dresser in the bedroom. Most importantly to Chris, there is a rather nice bookshelf in the living room. He can begin to actually get some used books to go with his "Count of Monte Cristo". For the first time in a long while he realizes that he has a few options.

Chris loves his job. He enjoys stocking the shelves and helping the part-time employee from the high school who likes to be called William, not Bill, but William. It looks like not everyone in this small town has escaped the temptation of putting on airs. But William is a good kid, and as strong as an ox which holds him in good stead when wrestling with one-hundred-pound feed bags. His parents probably put him up to that "William" stuff anyway, and he just might grow out of it in time.

The hardest part about Chris's job is dealing with people. He has always been a loner and, when in a conversation, he is a champion of the single-syllable response. He loves questions that can be answered by a simple yes or no. But he is learning to answer questions in a more comprehensive manner and to even make a bit of small talk. He has to. Dealing with the public is part of the job and so far he loves every other aspect of the work. So he tries being amiable and it's not that hard. He discovers that he has a dry wit and he tries it out from time to time with varying degrees of success. Most importantly, the folks who trade at Feltondale Hardware are not the abrupt wiseacres he's dealt with in the past. They are, for the most part, genuinely and naturally friendly. Not nosey, just friendly. Every day his banter with the town folk becomes easier and sometimes he feels that he actually has something worthwhile to add to a conversation. In fact, he's afraid that if he's not careful, he might become down-right gabby.

In the short time that he has lived in this town he feels safer and more at ease than anywhere he's ever lived. It's his intention to do everything he can to earn the trust and respect of the locals so he can keep it that way. That may seem like a laudable but unattainable goal, but it really is more of a lifelong process that will serve him well in the years to come.

As he enters the front door of the store at eight o'clock sharp on the last Monday of September, Dill welcomes him with his usual "It looks like a good morning doesn't it," to which Chris replies, "Boy howdy!" a rustic phrase he has picked up from the local ranchers. It seems to sum up the almost exuberant way he feels nowadays.

CHAPTER SEVEN ... 1962, THE PACIFIC

The brothers Daniels are having one hell of a good time shaping the galley on the *Stella del Sud* into the kind of place they can prepare the meals for the crew with the least amount of effort and the greatest degree of success. It turns out that keeping a bunch of rag-tag sailors satiated is not much of a tall order for two hard-working short-order cooks; especially if they are from the South where flavor is king and nutritional value doesn't even enter into the equation. The operative word in the sort of cuisine they have been taught is *fried*. For breakfast, fried eggs, fried bacon, fried sausage and ham, fried hush puppies, fried potatoes, and even fried bread in a pinch. If they could fry coffee, they would.

And what about that wonderful Southern belly-filler, grits. The first time a northerner sees a pile of grits on his plate he is surely disappointed. He can't see what all the fuss is about; after all it turns out when you boil it down, and that's exactly what you do, grits are just a white variety of cornmeal mush. Not much to recommend about them on their own. But ask any Southerner and she or he will tell you, "It ain't the grits by their own selves that's important, but what you puts on 'em that counts." Add a few select condiments and you have a mighty mush indeed.

Pour on some Karo syrup, salt and pepper, and add lots of butter, and simple grits become a mouth-watering treat. But what they don't tell you is that adding Karo Syrup, salt and pepper, and gobs of butter to almost anything, even boiled cardboard, should make it taste pretty damn good. But grits are cheaper, a lot easier to cook than cardboard, and a hell of a lot easier to digest.

And that's just the fried-ness of *breakfast*. Let's not forget the Southern dinner; fried chicken, with some kind of greens fried in chicken fat, and mashed potatoes and chicken-fat gravy. Even okra, an acquired taste for most, can liven up an ordinary meal when sautéed in fat.

So the brothers have quite an arsenal of culinary delights at their command, which is amazing as they are not even sure what culinary means. No, the only problem they face in the galley is the lack of raw materials. They are really limited in what they can serve by what is in the larder. But absence is another of invention's mothers, and they do quite well with what they have on hand. They discover you can make a meal out of anything as long as you cook it in lard, and add a lot of seasonings. The French have been doing it for years.

The boys really do well with chicken, but chicken is a rare commodity more than three or four days out from land. They'll have to see if they can get more at the next port and figure out a way to keep it longer.

Maybe they should buy some live chickens and raise them on board so they can have really fresh fowl.

They had not done the shopping for supplies in Hawaii as the Captain told them it might be too dangerous for them to show their faces on U.S. territory. In actuality the Captain didn't quite trust them yet. So they gave a list of the supplies they wanted to their able assistant Manny and they laid low. In the future things will be different they explain to Manny. They will accompany him ashore in the next port and Manny assures them that most of their requirements can be found in Fiji, or any other port for that matter, if they spread out and search carefully.

So far the crew has been complimentary of their cooking. Breakfast is no problem. They make great coffee in the big metal urn in the ship's mess. They add egg shells to the coffee grinds and a bit of chicory they found on the top shelf of the larder; another old Southern trick. They have what seems to be a year's supply of oatmeal and they'll be sure to get some raw sugar and Karo syrup at the next port if they can find it; not to mention grits. If they can't find Karo, then Yankee maple syrup will have to do, or some kind of island sugar-cane concoction. They can spice up the powdered eggs with salt and pepper, and chopped onions. There are plenty of cold cuts, cheese, and peanut butter for sandwiches at lunch time and they are able to bake a decent loaf of bread after several disastrous attempts.

And of course there is a large supply and variety of fish considering where they are, on the ocean and all. It is a standing rule that, if the fishing lines trailing the stern rail chance to catch any fish, it must be brought to the galley to be shared by all the crew. It is a great distance between ports where they can buy fresh meat of any kind, so any fish the crew can provide are a boon to the brothers in their attempt to provide some fresh food in the powdered this, and canned that, menu that they usually have to work with.

And fortunately, the crew never seems to tire of rice. Of course there is the steamed variety, most any fool can cook that, but Manny teaches them how to make passable fried rice using the ungodly powdered eggs with a few chopped onions and bits of left-over this and that.

So there are no serious complaints about the food other than one decidedly daft deck hand who jokingly demands prime rib and oysters Rockefeller for every meal. The brothers are sure he's never tasted either in his life.

But their big triumph is what they accomplish with the live pig that is acquired in Hawaii. After relieving it of its life, they carefully butcher the pig into its most delicious component parts. There are shoulder hams, bacon from the pork belly, and pork chops and pork roast from the loin. Not a cubic inch of that pig goes to waste including the trotters, the hocks, and even the lips and ears which, with all the rest of the trimmings, go into the spiced sausage the brothers concoct with

an old hand-powered meat grinder they find in the
back of a cabinet.

The brothers even devise a meat smoker made from
a scrubbed barrel and scrounged parts from the
engine room. Their smoke-cured bacon and ham is a
special Sunday treat that pleases the crew no end and
even has the Captain grinning. Overall, they succeed
in their "culinary" efforts far beyond what is expected
of them. Their Mama would be proud of what her two
wayward boys have achieved in their maritime
kitchen. And the Captain assures them that, if they
can keep up the good work and keep their noses
clean, the sharks and cops will surely be kept at bay.

They had told him that they could damn sure cook,
and they damn sure can.

CHAPTER EIGHT ...1953–1963, NEW YORK CITY

Penny loves Feltondale in her heart, but she has to admit it is rather insular. There isn't much in the town to stimulate a growing mind with the exception perhaps of the library. Maybe that's one of the reasons most of the young folk choose to leave right after high school and never come back except for visits in the summer for a week or so, or around the Holidays.

When she had gone to college in Helena there had been much more activity. There was live music, and theater, and a modicum of bustle due to the fact that it was the state capitol. But it was still, at its heart, Montana; Feltondale writ large. Helena was provincial, that's true, but it wasn't that there was no *there* there, as Gertrude Stein had described her hometown of Oakland, California. With both Feltondale and Helena it was as if there wasn't *supposed to be* a *there* there; and that was fine. There were never any pretensions of *there*ness.

So when Penny leaves Grand Central Station stepping into the mayhem that is midtown Manhattan, she is completely overwhelmed. There certainly is *there* there; lots of it, maybe too much *there*, way more than she thinks she can ever manage to comfortably handle.

She has brought just one suitcase on the chance that her interview doesn't work out but she should not have worried. The people at Guild Publishing are most cordial and show none of the haughtiness she was sure they would feel for a girl straight from the sticks. She only has one interview, with her future boss Emily Proctor, who is a senior editor at Guild and has a stable of writers that is quite impressive. Mrs. Proctor has two editors working for her, and three associate editors, but she needs an editorial assistant to help coordinate all of their activities and interface with the other departments of the publishing house and even outside vendors.

Emily Proctor had been a close friend of Lisa McCutcheon in college and her recommendation was really all that was needed to endorse Penny. The interview, after all her worries and preparation, is merely perfunctory. Penny has the job.

The first chance Penny gets after leaving the Guild offices she calls her father and Aunt Martha collect to share the good news with the two most important people in her life. Though she knows down deep they are broken hearted to lose their little girl again, she also knows that they understand that this is what she wants. At least, they are outwardly supportive. This, after all, is just another logical and almost inevitable step in her growth that began when she left Feltondale for the first time to go to college. But then she had been just hours away. Now they seem to be worlds apart.

And in many ways they are. Her father and Martha will not share in this world Penny is discovering as she becomes acquainted with the sensory overload that makes New York City the largest attraction and distraction in the world. Penny's experiences in New York will further separate her from her life in Feltondale.

She has conflicted thoughts about this whole business. She thinks of that familiar song from World War I; "How are you gonna keep 'em down on the farm, after they've seen Paree?" Or New York in this case. "Well maybe you can't keep 'em down on the farm but they can eventually come back to it if they so choose," she thinks. But for now, she decides that New York is going to be her oyster and Feltondale is just a part of her past; a place she has left behind. It will be a very long time before Penny realizes that you really *can't* take the country out of the girl; at least this one.

Penny asks her dad and Martha to send her a long list of things she absolutely needs to survive, as soon as they can via Railway Express. She'll pick them up when she has a place to live which hopefully won't take too long or be too painful a process. Until she can find a place, she is happy with her small room in a mid-town hotel that is near to the office and doesn't cost too much; at least for the short run.

Penny's new job is both a challenge and a delight. She is shocked to find that there are dozens of types and ranks of editors in the hierarchy of Guild Publishing. She, of course, starts at the bottom. She begins by learning how the publishing business works by mastering any number of rudimentary tasks. By working for several weeks in the mailroom, sorting and delivering the mail to all of the various departments from the top down, she quickly learns who is who, and basically what they do. She is then assigned to her own department as an editorial assistant in training.

In her mind, her future goal is to become an editor and have her own stable of writers to work with. But that is a long way off; if ever. For now, she has to focus on all of the things she has to learn about being an editor. She begins with simple administrative tasks such as filing and even a small amount of typing; though her skills in that area are far from top-drawer.

After a short while, she is ready to be a full-fledged editorial assistant where her duties are even more varied. It is still in a learning situation, but at a higher, more specific level. She supports the editorial staff in the multitude of activities necessary to put a book on a bookstore shelf; and eventually into a reader's hands. She begins summarizing written material and correcting manuscripts. She learns a little about issuing contracts, dealing with royalties, and a lot about scheduling and tasking. She interfaces with the production department, learning how to work with the designers, photographers, illustrators, and researchers. She learns to budget time and about the importance of deadlines. Most of the time she is exhausted at the end of the day, but she is almost always happy.

The most fun and rewarding of all of these tasks, is the first reading of unsolicited manuscripts. That chore always falls on the most junior member of the editorial staff. Most manuscripts are awful, but every once in a while there is a gem that she passes on to her superiors. One book that had begun with a reading by her is actually published and enjoys a modest success. She always considers it to be "her" manuscript and follows the author's modest endeavors throughout her life.

To each of her assignments she brings a fresh and open-minded acceptance. This is also true when it comes to the mysteries of the city itself. She lacks the blasé attitude that sophistication can engender, and it seems as if she spends most of her waking hours in a state of perpetual wonder.

On the job, she takes great pride and satisfaction in all that she learns and accomplishes and as a result she is a joy to work with. In short, her lowly position at Guild completely fulfills her vocational desires for the time being. But as usual, her private life is another matter.

Penny has been directed to the Wingate Arms Residence for Women which is only five blocks from work. It is a beautiful building with an impressive sandstone façade replete with wrought-iron lanterns on each side of the entryway. The vestibule is equally impressive, with large ornate Spanish-inspired couches lining the walls. However, the deeper you go into the building the more simple and less impressive it becomes.

But it is a safe haven for the single girls and women who are just starting out or who are reluctant to face the brashness of the big city.

There are only a few single rooms at the Wingate as most of them were designed for two people sharing a bath. It is very similar to a college dormitory with the exception of the age of the residents who are mostly in their mid to late twenties. Women exactly like Penny.

With your room you receive a bountiful bonus; there is, included in the weekly price of your room, a buffet-style breakfast every morning. That is a godsend. It sends Penny off to work each day well fed, adhering to the old adage that one should breakfast like a king, or a queen in this case. With a large breakfast tucked away, she can easily last until lunch which she usually eats in the company cafeteria. Dinner is another matter as cooking in the room is discouraged. This leaves her eating a lot of Italian or Chinese take-out in the room or stopping at inexpensive restaurants on the way home. All in all, Penny is glad to have such a stable environment what with the newness and challenge of her job and the overwhelming impact of New York City on her Montana sensibilities.

At first, she is disappointed that there are no single rooms available when she applies to the Arms. In retrospect however, she feels that what at first seemed to be a drawback is really a blessing in disguise. Her roommate turns out to be a girl from the West Coast. Her name is Sami Gilchrist and she has recently graduated from Stanford Law School. She is in a demanding internship at a prestigious law firm in mid-town Manhattan. She is a quiet and considerate roommate, as is Penny.

During the week, the both of them are exhausted from the rigors of their new and demanding jobs. With the stress of having to learn a myriad of new things, and the long work day, they have little time to do anything but eat and sleep in their off hours.

But on the weekends, especially Sunday, they drop their business mantels, leave the protection of the Wingate Arms and take off to roam all over the city. They quickly discover that the subway is great for getting to point B from point A but that there is little to view in the dark tunnels under the city. So they take to the streets. Often they just walk, but the busses are usually not overcrowded on a Sunday and they offer great views. It doesn't matter that they don't know what they are looking at. After all, just seeing the vibrant city from the moving bus window is a pleasure in, and of, itself.

They religiously take advantage of the free admission days at the many museums and entertainment venues in the city and on rare occasions they splurge on less expensive same-day matinee tickets to the ballet or the theater.

Both Penny and Sami had led active lives in their teens and the miles that they now walk each Sunday are a welcome change from their sedentary weekday endeavors. They get, in one day, the exercise that their entire busy weekday schedules preclude. And the physical activity seems to clear their heads. When they climb in their beds on Sunday night, they know they will awaken refreshed and ready to tackle the stress and strain of another week of work. Penny grows to love her life in New York City both at work and, for once, at play.

And then a change moves Penny in a new direction; Sami leaves the Wingate. A fellow intern at the law firm has found a small two–bedroom apartment but can't afford the steep rent without a roommate. She invites Sami to join her and Sami can't pass up the opportunity to have a "real" place to live and a chance to cook and eat meals at home. She leaves Penny with regret; but she leaves never-the-less.

Penny's new roommate, Jeanie, turns out not to be as ideal as Sami. Jeanie has a boyfriend and is not interested in doing anything with Penny on the weekends. The change leaves Penny looking for an opportunity to move into an apartment like Sami has. After all, if she really wants to be a New Yorker with a capital NY, then she needs to live somewhere more permanent than what is essentially a glorified boarding house. She decides that her days at the Wingate Arms are numbered. But when she scours the newspapers and the bulletin boards at work for a place to live, by the time she answers the ads the places are invariably gobbled up.

Then one day, when she has come to the conclusion that she is never going to find a proper place to live, she overhears a conversation in the cafeteria that changes everything. At the next table are three young women, around her age, discussing how hard it is to survive in New York City especially with the lack of reasonable apartments in areas that are safe places to live. The girl closest to Penny, but with her back to her, is the most vocal on the subject. Her roommate has just gotten married and moved out leaving her with rent she can't afford. She needs to find a new roommate right away. She doesn't have the luxury of having the time to properly find the perfect roommate. She has the upcoming rent to pay. But she is very particular about the type of person she lives with. They have to be neat and considerate and it wouldn't hurt if they share some of the same interests. She loves to roam around the city on her days off. Her last roommate enjoyed that too, until she met her man and that was the end of that. But most of all she needs a roommate in a hurry.

Penny has to make a choice; admit that she has been eaves dropping and run the risk of alienating the girl, or find some other way to approach her. She slowly turns around and sees that the other girls are leaving but her possible future roommate is still seated. She swallows her pride and makes her move without any further thought.

"Excuse me," she says, "I couldn't help but overhear your conversation." She is embarrassed, not by the intrusion and eavesdropping admission, but that she has chosen such a hackneyed phrase to introduce herself. Thankfully the girl is not offended and has a quizzical smile on her face that prompts Penny to add, "You see, I think I have the solution to your predicament. You are looking for a roommate and I know someone who meets all of your requirements; namely, me."

And so Penny finds a place to live and a kindred soul to share it with; a friend to replace Sami.

Penny's new apartment is about ten blocks from work. On nice days, when they have fifteen minutes or so to spare she, and her new roommate, Grace, walk to the Guild Publishing offices. Grace works in the royalty accounting department so their jobs rarely overlap. But they meet for lunch in the cafeteria on Fridays as a treat. The rest of the week they brown-bag it which is, after all, one of the advantages of having your own kitchen.

Penny resumes her Sundays in and around the city, this time with Grace who has many new perspectives to offer for Penny's consideration. She introduces Penny to the magic of the Cloisters in the farthest northern reaches of Manhattan. To avoid the long drab subway ride they take the still longer but infinitely more scenic M4 bus ride all the way from mid-town to the faraway location to the north.

The Cloisters is just that; an assemblage of actual elements of five medieval cloisters, disassembled and shipped from southern France and joined together again to create what appears to be a unified medieval setting. It is located in an enchanting spot perched on a bluff overlooking the Hudson River. There are tranquil gardens planted according to horticultural information found in medieval treatises on medicine.

It is a branch of the Metropolitan Museum of Art and is the home of approximately three thousand works of art from medieval Europe, dating from the ninth to the sixteenth century, including exquisite illuminated manuscripts, stained glass, metalwork, enamels, ivories, and tapestries. In this setting, they seem to come alive and give the rooms the air of an actual place where people could live and not just a museum you can only visit.

But most importantly to Penny and Grace, it is a respite from the hectic pace of the rest of New York; a place to recharge your batteries by stepping back in time to enjoy a more simple and peaceful world. The young women go there when they can.

After a year on the job Penny has a good grasp of how the company functions in general and the inner workings of the editorial department in particular. She is given a small cubicle and promoted to be Mrs. Proctor's fourth associate editor. She continues to read manuscripts, but not all are unsolicited. Her input is valued to a greater degree by her associates and superiors. It won't be long she feels before she will become a full-fledged editor. It actually takes three more years but when she is finally promoted she is more than fully prepared.

In her second year as an editor she makes her first real coup. It comes about under rather unusual circumstances. She and Grace have wandered into a coffee house in Greenwich Village late one Saturday night and are taken aback by the engaging power of a young man at the mike on a postage-stamp stage. He is reciting an earthy, raw, and sometimes downright raunchy poem. After hearing several such pieces Penny comments that she feels that it isn't his presentation that is so remarkable and engaging but the material itself.

As if it was preordained, he approaches their table after he is through with his performance and asks if he can join them. His name is Anthony Weston and he has lived in the Village for two years. He is tall, dark, and muscular and wears a plaid shirt, Levi's, and tan boots; as if Jack Kerouac had moved east. If they ever need a lumberjack in the Village they don't have far to look. But to Penny and Grace he is both fascinating and a little bit overwhelming due to his unbridled and unexpurgated enthusiasm for life.

The three of them talk for what seems just a short while in the nearly deserted coffee house but when they open the front door and emerge into the city they are shocked to find that the sun has beaten them to it.

Anthony is conversant in a variety of subjects and he is remarkably well rounded if somewhat self-centered. When he learns that Penny is an editor he mentions that he has just finished a novel about his experiences in the Village. He asks if Penny would take a look at it. Against her rule of not reading unsolicited works outside of the office she acquiesces. They make a date to meet for dinner later in the day at a small mid-town Italian restaurant. This time Anthony is dressed less like Paul Bunyan and more in keeping with city life; dark pants and a black turtleneck. It makes him even more attractive and somewhat mysterious to Penny. After a leisurely and delightful dinner, and probably too much wine, they split the bill and go out on the sidewalk. After carefully considering the ramifications, Penny accepts Anthony's offer to escort her home. They walk slowly as if they want the evening to last. Anthony is carrying a shopping bag that contains a copy of his manuscript.

When they reach the front steps of Penny's apartment house, it seems that Anthony has lost his usual sense of bravado and he quietly thanks Penny for the wonderful evening without the awkward, kiss or no kiss, rigmarole. Anthony hands her the bag, and walks off into the night. It is almost as if he is a little afraid of her. Maybe the edgy persona he projects is merely a ruse to hide a more sensitive nature.

Penny is relieved, but also puzzled, at this other side of him.

They have agreed to meet the next Saturday night at the coffee house and she hopes she will have had a chance by then to have read some of the manuscript. This is a huge underestimation of what is to occur.

From the moment she begins reading she is hooked. His writing is unaffected and unpretentious. He pulls no punches. The book is a vital and vivid portrayal of life in Greenwich Village, or at least it is from Penny's naïve point of view. It is sometimes so sensual and explicit that the Montana part of Penny is shocked. Even after living in New York for six years, she often blushes at his preposterous prose and almost pornographic depiction of the sexual mores of the village. But his book is real. It is powerful. And, most important, it is hers.

She realizes that it needs a lot of work but after all she is an editor trained in the art of making literature more accessible and therefore more saleable. But she is sure that she can edit it without interfering with the thrust and tone of the work.

The first hurdle is to get the book into proper shape to present to the senior editor. The second is to talk Guild, a very conservative house, into publishing such a risqué novel. The first will just take work. The second may take an act of God.

On their next meeting Penny enthusiastically endorses Anthony's work and offers to edit the book with him so as to make it presentable for publication.

Anthony recognizes that this is an opportunity he can't pass up. He also realizes he is growing very fond of Penny but that he must control his passions in case they might interfere with her work on the book. Without even knowing it, Penny has nipped a romance in the bud.

Over the next two months Penny and Anthony work together on the project. The working title is "The Village" which seems perfectly appropriate to Penny. It would seem at the outset that this is the only part of the book upon which they can agree. The struggle between writer and editor is dynamic and strenuous; especially for the first-time author of such a radical book. Penny must be careful not to change the power of Anthony's prose and Anthony must conform to a few accepted literary conventions if he hopes to have his book published. A strain is put on their friendship but the hours working closely together are beneficial as well. They come out the other side of the sometimes painful editing process with not only a saleable book but with a high regard for each other's talents.

With the editing process completed Anthony removes the self-imposed restraints he has placed on their relationship and tries to take it to a more romantic level. The hard work they have expended on the book has earned them a strong sense of closeness and trust. Can romance be far away? Anthony hopes so but it would be so much easier for him to progress, if he were aware that Penny feels the same way. She is more introverted and hard to read but the effort that they poured into the book is now directed toward each other; with the inevitable results.

One Sunday afternoon Anthony and Penny return from a late breakfast and a long walk to discover a note from Grace on the refrigerator. Since Monday is a holiday, she has accepted an impromptu invitation from a friend to visit his brother in Baltimore. She'll be back in time for dinner Monday night.

As in the commission of a crime, motive, means, and opportunity, are suddenly present for Penny and Anthony and they find that it is completely natural for them to take their relationship to its logical conclusion. Friends become lovers bathed in the warm afternoon sun coming through the window of Penny's bedroom.

But the morning light finds them both wondering about what had just happened. Not if they did the right thing; after all they are adults and it was a magical moment. But they both are not sure that they are desirous of anything like a permanent commitment. They decide to keep their new-found relationship a secret until they both can come to a conclusion about whether this is what they really want. Maybe they are ruining a perfect friendship by adding an unnecessary new ingredient into the mix; no matter how delightful. Most importantly, it is time for Penny to focus entirely on getting Anthony's novel published by Guild.

Her first step is to submit it, with a strong endorsement, to the senior editor for fiction, Gregory Campbell Drummond. Drummond is a soft-spoken man who would seem more at home in the halls of academe than in the business world. But he is a canny judge of what will sell and what won't. Plus, he is willing to take risks, on occasion, to support a manuscript he is really fond of. Penny is hoping that "The Village" will be just such a book.

The wait for a decision on the book is almost unbearable. So much hangs in the balance. Not just the risk to her stature as an editor by having made such a strong, unequivocal endorsement, but the creative investment that Anthony has made in writing this gutsy portrayal of life in New York's Bohemia in the first place, and the long and sometimes painful hours they both have put into editing his momentous work.

Finally, a week later on a Friday afternoon, Penny is summoned to Drummond's corner office. She sits on a chair in front of his desk hoping for the best, but prepared for the worst.

"Well Penny, it would appear that you have got yourself a handful with this monster of a novel. Where did you ever find it?" he begins and then continues not waiting for an answer.

"I was both enthralled and appalled by this book. I love it and I know it has an audience but my first response was, 'Are we the ones to publish it?' After all, Guild is an old, conservative publishing house.

We are not known for our risk taking, or risqué taking as it is in this case. This was my predicament when I read this wonderful and exciting book but there might be a solution.

I ran this dilemma by the editor-in-chief, Kenneth Edmonds, and I think he has come up with something that will get this published and still protect our pristine image. He wanted to tell you himself but he has been called out of the office and passed the pleasure on to me.

So here's the deal. As you know, the courts have recently decided that 'Lady Chatterley's Lover' and 'The Tropic of Cancer' are not obscene since they have overriding literary value. Both Edmonds and I think 'The Village' would fall into that category as well."

"Thank God," Penny blurts out.

"But we aren't out of the woods yet. Even if the courts would clear the explicit nature of parts of this book, publishing it under the Guild name would not be in our best interests when you think of our exalted image. So, here's the solution; why Edmonds gets the big bucks by the way.

You must surely know that we have a subsidiary in Paris by the name of Liberte Press. They handle the translation, sales, and distribution of our titles in France and the French speaking world, what there is left of it. We do the same for them in the English speaking world." Drummond pauses and Penny sits as still as if she were in a trance waiting for him to continue. She is afraid that any movement on her part would somehow break the spell.

"Well, the plan that the chief came up with is brilliant, I must say. We will have Liberte publish the book in Paris, and we will handle the distribution in the English speaking world. We are majority owners of Liberte so most of the profits, if any, will come to us. Any headaches and negativity will hopefully accrue to Liberte. It's a 'have your cake and eat it too' situation." He pauses with a grin, "I'm sorry. What do you think Penny? You're sitting there like a statue. I haven't let you get but two words in edgewise."

Penny is so flabbergasted she takes a long time to reply. She can think of a thousand things to say but settles with a simple reply.

"I think it is genius, Mr. Drummond; pure genius. What can I do to help?"

"Well, the first thing we need to do is sign up our aspiring young author. You'll have to go to legal and get a contract set up with Liberte and all. Then you'll have to explain the set up to the author and get him to sign on to it. Then, with our contract in hand, we can proceed to send a copy of the manuscript to Paris and start the ball roulez-ing. N'est pas?"

"I can't thank you enough Mr. Drummond," Penny exclaims as she rises from her seat.

"No need for thanks; just action. Let's get this done! Give me progress reports as you go along and bring in this Anthony fellow so I can meet him and make him welcome into our stable."

This is the highpoint in Penny's New York career. It establishes her as an editor to be reckoned with. Anthony's book is an international success; however, as often is the case, his subsequent endeavors can't quite live up to its stellar performance. But their romantic involvement slowly comes to an end. Just what they feared has taken place. Their friendship is in jeopardy. Penny is too valuable as his friend and editor. Anthony is too valuable as her friend and client. So they agree to continue their relationship on a strictly friend and client basis. Some times less is more.

After a decade, she has hit the glass ceiling that is especially prevalent at this time in the publishing business. One day, glancing at the bulletin board in the cafeteria she sees a for-sale sign for a second-hand Oldsmobile station wagon offered by a production supervisor who lives in the suburbs.

This simple sign sets off a chain of events that cannot be reversed. The car represents freedom to Penny. She has a well-stocked savings plan and goes home with the car's owner that very night and tests the car. It seems perfect. She pays the man what he asks for it on the stipulation that she can leave it at his house for at least two weeks. This purchase accelerates her plan. She realizes the bustle of New York has lost its charm. She has accomplished everything she set out to do; even more. The simple life of her childhood beckons to her.

When she turns in her notice, everyone at Guild is shocked and extremely sorry that she is leaving. So to help mitigate the loss she is asked if she would like to continue her association with Guild as a free-lance editor. They hate to be without her services completely. This will allow her to work on a project-by-project basis from anywhere she chooses.

She chooses Montana. She picks up her Oldsmobile, packs up the belongings she wants to take, and heads west.

CHAPTER NINE ... 1955-1962, WASHINGTON, D.C.

Wes spends more than a year overseas. Not the Pacific but the Atlantic.

He travels throughout the varied lands of Europe and is amazed at the diversity of styles and customs. It is compact. There are few great expanses; just delightful vistas. The cities and towns are vastly different than anything he has ever experienced in the United States. And no matter the country or ethnic group, he is usually pleasantly charmed by the people.

He especially loves the small villages in England and is entranced with Scotland and Ireland which are his ancestral homes. But he is taken aback at the devastation the blitz has caused in London. So many of the old buildings are gone and many of the buildings that have replaced them are ugly, unharmonious, utilitarian structures that he senses will not wear well over the years.

Rome, to Wes, is a magical place though he sometimes finds some of the Italians themselves to be less than forthright and often just plain annoying. Saint Peter's is overwhelming in its magnitude and expansive splendor. The food he loves the most is remarkably simple and equally honest, and, of course, delicious.

And then there is Paris. This is the most beautiful city he has ever seen. Every block is an outdoor museum. The uniform and elegant design of the townhouses, streets, and buildings that give Paris its charm are, in the main, he learns, the result of the inspired city planning of Baron Haussmann. He rebuilt Paris in the mid 1800's at the behest of Napoleon III. It might have been the original object to create the broad boulevards to be able to move troops more easily, but in accomplishing that military objective, Haussmann actually succeeded in creating what the world loves most about the French capital. Haussmann cut through the old crowded Paris of dense and irregular medieval alleys, and turned it into a gracefully monumental city with wide avenues, open spaces, and grand vistas. Wes is in love with the City of Light. He spends over a year, on and off, in Paris. His favorite quarter is the area around Saint Germain de Pres on the left bank. It seems like a small town in the midst of the grander, more monumental Paris. If you stuck Feltondale in the middle of Chicago, you'd get the same result. Sort of.

Ever organized and purposeful, Wes attempts to give himself a liberal-arts education to make up for the university subjects he had not taken as a result of his intense study of the law. He goes to every museum he can find and develops his own art history course studying and organizing what he sees and reads into a cohesive package of information he feels comfortable with. It seems to him that he has become at least a little bit cultured. Maybe it doesn't show, but it is there and available should he ever need it; sort of like all of the miles of minutiae he learned in law school.

But after several years in Europe he feels that he is ready to return to America, maybe not to Montana yet, but perhaps New York or Chicago. And he knows he needs to visit Washington, D.C. and spend at least a small portion of the time in his capital, that he has spent visiting all the capitols of Europe. He lands in New York in the fall of 1957 and is immediately uneasy. Paris is still fresh in his mind. And New York suffers by comparison in his eyes. He determines that he is not ready for another huge metropolis, especially as overwhelming and alienating as he figures New York can be. So he decides to go directly to Washington, D.C. After all, there is still plenty of money in the trust fund his grandfather had left for him. Why not spend it on something both useful and fun? This may be his only chance. He is quite pleased with what he finds in the nation's capital. It has some of the charm and monumentality of Paris, Rome, and even London. And it is *his* capital, not some foreign city. Something in his background tells him that he should become more than merely acquainted with Washington, D.C. so he continues the alternative education that he had begun in Paris; but this time it is American History 101, not art. It is his plan to stay a week. He stays almost six years.

One chilly day, when the fall colors are just beginning to wane, and shortly after his arrival in Washington, D.C. he wanders into a large, impressive building that houses the offices of some of the representatives that serve in the Congress. On the orientation directory in the lobby he comes across a name he is familiar with, Richard Weaver. The name rings a bell. The first thing he remembers about him was that you never call him "Dick". He had met a Richard Weaver at Yale Law. Richard was a year ahead of Wes and had been active in all sorts of campus politics and the like. Wes had gone to a few rallies for this and that but he had never been very political himself, even as a political science major in his undergraduate years. He remembers Weaver as an earnest and engaging fellow. And most of all he remembers him because he is from Montana. This must be the same guy. While Wes was wandering around Europe on his Grand Tour, Weaver has become a Congressman from Montana. Montana's two Senators are for some inexplicable reason liberal Democrats but the letter in parenthesis next to Weaver's name is "R".

Wes doesn't think twice. He locates the office in the maze-like structure and enters it. The outer office is wood paneled and suitably impressive. There are western-themed prints on the wall and the chairs and sofa are leather. Behind the desk is an older, very attractive, woman who appears to be the epitome of composure.

"May I help you, Sir?" she asks.

"Yes of course, is the Congressman in? My name is Wes Felton and I'm from Montana. I think that Richard and I were at Yale Law at the same time", Wes replies.

"Congressman Weaver is on the floor right now. They're taking a vote on a mining bill and he is one of the co-sponsors. He should be back soon. He has a pretty full calendar today but you may wait if you like; so you can say hello," she says carefully, walking the fine line between protecting the Congressman's time and not offending a visiting constituent. Well done, Wes thinks. She is a jewel.

"Thanks, I'll wait a few minutes and see if he comes back," Wes says as he sits in the overstuffed leather chair and grabs a copy of the National Geographic. He remembers as a kid looking for any feature stories on Africa in case there were some photos of African women au naturale. Their rarely were. Just as he is about to leave, the door flies open, and the whirlwind that is Richard Weaver enters the room. He looks at Wes as if he might recognize him. To save face for both of them Wes, speaks quickly.

"Hi Richard, I'm Wes Felton from Yale Law. You were in the class ahead of me. I met you a couple of times at various political things."

"Yes, Wes I remember. You were at that Stevenson rally and a bunch of us went into town for too many beers afterward. You're from Montana, right?" he asks moving across the room to shake Wes's hand.

"So what brings you to the seat of power? You need a dam built or new post office in your town? You've come to the right man," Richard says. "Come on in to my office and let's catch up," he continues turning to his gate keeper, "Let me know when Senator Moore gets here will you, Trudi."

"Sit down Wes I've got a few minutes to chat," Richard says as he sits behind his desk and motions Wes to the straight-back chair at the side of the desk. "So, what's up Wes? Are you just visiting or have you come out here to give me a hand?" he says with a grin.

"Well, I've just spent a few years in Europe. I went back to Feltondale to practice with my dad after law school and I stayed there for a couple of years but my heart just wasn't in it. So I took a sabbatical. I came to D.C. just to invest some of my interest in my own country after soaking up all that decadent European culture. And what do you mean give you a hand? You seem to be doing fine," Wes states looking around the room at all the framed photos of Richard posing with imposing people.

"I don't exactly know, Wes, it's still in the formulation stage. I guess you can tell I am kind of impulsive. I get hunches quite often and I act on them a lot of the time. Lucky for me, they've been mostly right. When you sat down I had a flash thought that you might be looking for a job. Who knows, maybe you are, and you just don't know it yet," Weaver pauses and leans back in his chair as if he were about to say something important and needed to gather his thoughts. "You probably don't remember the Legislative Reform Act of 1946. Why would you? It was important to the folks around here but I bet it didn't make much of a splash in Montana. Anyway, it gave Congress the money to have larger, more productive, staffs; doing research on bills, offering legal advise and the like. I just came here in January and I haven't been able to get a full staff yet.

I know it sounds abrupt but I'm in the market for a legal advisor to work with me on a number of issues. The advisor from my predecessor stayed on while he lined up a new job, but he just went back to join a practice in Helena and I'm now in the market for a legal eagle. I know it's a long shot but are you by any chance, ready to turn in your traveling shoes and give up your guise as a professional vagabond? Are you looking to put down a few roots; at least for a little while? The pay is lousy but it's a chance to learn how this government works or doesn't work. Any chance you'd be at all interested?"

Wes is bowled over. "My God Richard, you're serious. You sure do take your time to think things through; don't you. You know, at first thought, I just might be interested. I'm not ready to settle down back in Feltondale, and I'm about traveled out. I'd need a while to think about it. I'm intrigued and it is very tempting. And I'm impulsive like you. I follow hunches as well. What's say we talk about this after you get finished with your day?"

"Sure, Wes. That would be great and I'm glad your tempted. I'll be done here about 6:30. Why don't you meet me over at the bar in the Willard. If nothing comes of our conversation you'll at least get to see D.C.'s most famous watering hole. Walk around a while, take stock, and think it over. Just let the city work some more of its magic on you. I'll see you there."

And so Wes finds a job he wasn't looking for and spends the next six years as a congressional aide and legal counsel. He works on a host of fasinating projects; some of which actually become laws. Most effect the health and wealth of Montana directly but others deal with national issues. It is a learning experience that is invaluable.

But when Richard Weaver decides not to run in 1962 Wes sees it as a sign that, he too, is through with Washington, D.C. It is finally time to go home to stay. He has a wealth of knowledge about how to get things done in the political and governmental arena and he is anxious to see if he can apply his hard earned skills on a local level to help the town of Feltondale, his namesake, to survive and maybe even thrive.

It is finally time to retire his valise and settle down. His dad will be happy to have him back, and to tell you the truth, he'll be happy to be the "and Son" again.

CHAPTER TEN ... 1962, THE PACIFIC

It is hard to fathom just how deep the blue of the Pacific really is, especially it seems, south of the equator. The Daniels brothers never cease to be amazed at the mesmerizing color. Standing at the stern rail of the *Stella* they are taking a smoke break between breakfast and lunch. So far their time on the ship has been good. They have the galley running smoothly and the crew seems to be happy with the results of their efforts. But now they are in the midst of a secret project that might get them in a heap of trouble. They never have known when to leave well enough alone. Nobody ever taught them how to stay out of trouble, though to quote Merle Haggard," Momma Tried." And they haven't the mental where-with-all to figure it out on their own.

On an expedition down below to the engine room, looking for anything that could be used to fabricate their meat smoker, they had noticed a large coil of copper tubing in what appeared to be a seldom used storage locker. It was laying there all coiled up as if it were ready to strike. The discovery of the coil of copper tubing sparks an idea in both the brothers that grabs hold of their somewhat limited imaginations.

"Do you think we can scrounge enough spare parts from around the ship to make us a still?" John asks Charles as they toss their cigarette butts over the stern rail and mosey back to the galley.

"I don't know for sure, but maybe. You're thinkin' about that copper tubing ain't you? I know, 'cause I have been too; ever since we saw it in that locker," Charles replies and then appears to be thinking. "Well, for starters, what we need is a pressure cooker. That's the easiest thing to make a small still out of. And we need some kind of bucket to put the copper coil in to cool the steam. You know brother, it just might be doable."

"The first thing we need to do is to liberate that copper tubing from that musty old engine-room locker. A bucket's a bucket; there are plenty of those we can borrow. And, come to think of it, there's an old pressure cooker on a top shelf in the larder. But I don't know if it works. Guess we'd better check it out before we do anything else," Charles offers.

"There's something you're forgetting, big brother. Even if we get it all assembled and working, what do we do about the smell? It's hard enough to hide the smell of a still in a holler, let alone on a ship," John interjects as they sit down at the mess table with a cup of coffee from the giant urn.

"I hadn't thought of that. I guess we'll have to ventilate it real good to get rid of the smell. Think we can do that John?"

"Manny would know how to do that," John states.

100

"Hell, I forgot about our little buddy. Your right, we're gonna need him to help. And we sure can't pull this off if we have to hide our operation from him. We gotta get him on our side. He's a gamer. I bet he'll want to play. Let's see what he has to say for himself."

They find Manny in the galley chopping onions for dinner and crying his eyes out. After explaining their project to him his onion tears turn into tears of joy.

"You know bosses, it's a great idea. And I wanna be part of it. But how do we make a still out of that old pressure cooker?" Manny excitedly asks.

"First we gotta make sure it works Manny. We don't want to blow up the place. If it holds pressure okay, then we take the valve out of the top and put a cork in the hole. We get that copper tubing from the engine room locker and coil it around a pickle jar or some big cylinder thing until we have a coil with about ten or so loops. Then we drill a hole in the cork a tiny bit smaller than the diameter of the copper tubing and force one end of the copper pipe into the cork. Then we run the coil into the cooling bucket and out the other end and we have a still." Charles explains but Manny still has a rather blank look on his face.

"It's really easy, Manny. Trust me. Here's how it works. You'll get it. Don't worry. First, we ferment a little bit of some sugary juice in a jar and change the sugar into not-so-strong alcohol. We'll get to that later. Then we put the fermented juice, which is called

101

the 'wash' for some reason, in the pressure cooker. The heat in the pressure cooker turns the alcohol in the fermented juice to steam, and then it pushes it up the copper tube. The coil that is in the bucket is cooler and when the alcohol vapors go through it they change back into a liquid and that comes out the end of the tube into a bottle. By then, the alcohol is a lot purer; and stronger. It's ready to age for a couple of minutes and then down the hatch, as the sailors say."

"That don't sound so easy, boss," Manny comments, "but if you say you can do it I believe you. Count me in."

"Welcome aboard the good ship moonshine Manny; let's go see if that pressure cooker works."

The dinner that night consists of boiled beef in gravy. It is cooked in only twenty minutes. The pressure cooker works. They are in business; at least mechanically. They retrieve the copper tubing from the engine room that night and find a ten-gallon syrup container for the cooling bucket.

The next items on their scavenger hunt are the raw materials. Charles explains the next step in the process to Manny the following day.

"First, we have to gather some ingredients to make what I told you yesterday is called the 'wash'. We need some kind of sugary or starchy juice that we can seal up in a jar with yeast to ferment for a couple of weeks or until it stops bubbling. That's when the sugar or starch in the 'wash' has been turned into weak-strength alcohol. Not strong like whiskey but more like wine or beer. We run that fermented stuff through the still to distill it into almost pure alcohol like I explained. We can make the 'wash' out of almost anything that has sugar or starch in it. We can use, plain sugar for plain alcohol, sugar cane for rum, wine for brandy; corn for moonshine, and grain for a whisky. And potatoes make a mean vodka. It'll be easy. What do you think John, what can we use for this test 'wash'?"

"Plain old sugar is the simplest thing we have to make our first 'wash' with. That will make alcohol but it won't taste very good. Do you think we can get any molasses in the next port for a better 'wash' and make some rum?" John asks his assembled moonshine crew.

"Hell bosses, these islands out here are where you get sugar cane from so it shouldn't be too hard to get some molasses. And sailors love their rum don't they."

"I'm not sure about all sailors, but I know pirates sure do," John responds. "So we gotta get started. I'm anxious to see if this works."

"Okay, let's make our trial run with a sugar 'wash'. We've got plenty of sugar and we've got yeast. When we're done maybe we can disguise the taste with some pineapple juice.

We can set up the still in the second storeroom. But we need ventilation 'cause the whole process stinks to high heaven," Charles states looking at Manny. He is quick to answer.

103

"I'll figure something out boss, don't you worry I can blow that smell away. I'll rig a fan up in the storeroom port hole. And it should be safe. We keep that room under lock and key anyway to keep the snackers out. It'll do just fine."

It starts out fine but it doesn't end up that way; or maybe, on second thought, it does.

The fermentation goes without a hitch and pretty soon they have their "wash". They set up the still and after a lot of trial and error get the thing running. High-proof alcohol drips out of the end of the copper tubing to everyone's delight. It has a sweet, cloying kind of medicinal taste but with the addition of some pineapple juice it is not only palatable but almost tasty; a tropical cocktail fit for the biggest kahuna.

And the ventilation scheme goes fine at first. They rig a fan in the porthole that sucks the foul air out of the room. The air extracted by the fan is blown outside along the side of the ship to the stern by the force of the wind that the ship's forward motion creates. But, they are going through a long stretch of the doldrums. Other than that generated by the ship, there is no natural wind at all. Everything is fine. But then a light breeze comes across the starboard quarter of the bow and lifts the moonshine laden air upwards, right into the open porthole of First Mate Mike Dolan's cabin. It gathers there and waits for him to return. When he opens the door the smell almost knocks him over. As his cabin is above the galley he thinks he knows where the smell has originated and immediately goes down below to investigate.

All three of the probable culprits are working on the evening meal in the galley when the First Mate appears. From the look on his face they know that something is terribly wrong. It could be that the jig is up. But they just keep chopping; what else can they do?

"Well, lads, what do we have here? There's a smell in my cabin that is worse than the stinkiest toilet in the lowest dive in the Orient. And it seems to be coming from your bailiwick. Do you have any idea what it could be?" Dolan asks.

The three cooks try to look more dumbfounded than they usually do. Not being masters of the quick, or even the slow, retort they just stand mute hoping Dolan will go away. He doesn't.

"I don't see anything here that looks like it could be the origin of that smell. Do you think we ought to check the storeroom mateys? Let's have a look. Fetch me the key if you would be so kind."

Charles takes the storeroom key out of his pocket and reluctantly hands it to Dolan without saying a word. Dolan takes the key, opens the door of the storeroom and goes inside. He comes out in under a minute.

"You didn't really think that hiding that still behind the potato sacks would keep a smart Irish fellow like me from finding it, do you? I assume the smell in my cabin comes from a recent use of that jury-rigged piece of almost-machinery. I bet you were making a batch of potable poteen; moonshine to you. Am I wrong?" The boys stand mute but bow their heads. They mumble "No Sir" as they have been trained to do but Dolan doesn't hear it.

"I assume by your silence that I am right in my observation. I also assume that you must have a jar or two of the result of your devious efforts. Would they be in the cooler? Why don't one of you fetch one, and we'll take it up to the Captain and see what he has to say about your little project."

They select a jar of the raw illicit elixir from the refrigerator to bring along as evidence. As they leave the galley Manny has the good sense to grab the can of pineapple juice out of the cooler as well

They climb up to the bridge to face the Captain as if they were mounting a hangman's scaffold.

After the First Mate explains what he has discovered, the Captain looks as though he is about to erupt. But then a sorrowful, almost mournful look appears on his face. That changes into a reluctant smile. He has run the gamut of his emotional responses when he finally addresses the contrite brothers and the terrified Manny.

"Well boys, it looks like you've started something you can't finish. Bring that jar over here and let me see what you've created."

He pours a finger or two of moonshine into his empty coffee cup and slowly brings it to his lips. Manny reacts immediately. He steps forward and proffers the can of pineapple juice pouring a little into the mug.

"Here Captain, you'll want to add a little of this stuff to improve the taste."

The Captain takes a sip. And then another. Then he drains the mug. His whole face lights up in an almost rapturous grin.

"My God boys, you damn sure can cook; in more ways than one. You know, I think you've created something that we can not only enjoy from time to time, but that we can sell on the open, or not so open, market. I'm impressed. Let's go down to the galley and see your operation. I'm sure there are a lot of improvements that can be made with the process. With an investment in better equipment and raw materials we might just be able to turn this old tub into a floating gold mine. I smell opportunity knocking. Lead the way to the still; I want to see what you've come up with to create the fine beverage that is intoxicating me in every sense of that wonderful word."

CHAPTER ELEVEN ... 1962, MONTANA

Wes can't believe how happy he is to be home; not just for a visit but permanently. He eagerly relinquishes his life as a vagabond.

During his travels, and his life in Washington, D.C., he had visited his home town when he could; on holidays and sometimes when he had time to take a vacation. He was happy to visit with his dad and even with his mom, and with the few friends from his childhood that were still living in and around Feltondale.

He would sit with his dad in their law offices and be brought up to date on the happenings at the family practice. He always felt a little guilty at seeing the brass plaque that proudly proclaimed that this was the home of "Felton and Son, Attorneys at Law." That sign had been there since the late nineteenth century and it never failed to bring a feeling of pride to Wes every time he saw it. On a recent visit, it had prompted him to remind his dad that he was just taking a leave of absence and would be back some time in the near future to take over his share of the business. His dad always replied, "I'll believe it when you bring more than one suitcase home. The practice will be here when you get that itch outta your hitch; and the sooner the better."

Wes's happiest times on his infrequent visits were when he grabbed his fly-fishing gear and headed out to the Clark Ranch where you could find, to his mind, the best fly-fishing spot in Montana; and therefore the world.

As the entrance road to the ranch passes over the metal bridge about three miles from the highway, you come to a place where the river is slow and shallow. But it is pocked with deep holes where reluctant trout wait for Wes to tempt them with his large assortment of home-made flies.

Reed Clark's oldest son Mitchell was one of Wes's closest friends in his youth. Wes and Mitchell had dated sisters in high school; Ruth and Rebecca. Ruth and Wes were a couple throughout high school and everyone thought that they were destined to marry at some point. However, when Wes went off to World War II, Ruth moved to Baltimore with her parents and Wes eventually lost touch with her altogether. Rebecca married Mitchell shortly after graduation.

Wes had a standing invitation to fish the river on the Clark Ranch anytime he wanted; even if Mitchell or his little sister Marge, who was ten years younger than him and a real nuisance, weren't around or were too busy to join him. Wes knew the combination to the locked gate that was about a quarter mile up the entrance road from the highway. The numbers were Mitchell's birthday. Wes always closed and carefully locked the gate behind him even though there was a cattle guard across the gateway. Better safe.

Mitchell Clark had taken over the day-to-day operation of the ranch from his dad who was semi-retired; which is about all the amount of retired you can be from a working ranch. There are just too many distractions that prevent you from completely letting go in the ranching business. That is unless you just pick up and leave, and Reed Clark would never do that. Marge, the little sister, had gone off to college in Texas. And Mitchell and Rebecca stayed home and were busy running the ranch. He had his father's love of the land and pride in the herd of Angus they ran on it. They were both destined to be lifers in the beef trade.

Wes made it a practice of only catching as many fish as he could eat or reasonably give away. The idea of "catch and release", or "maim and kill" as he called it, was abhorrent to him. Fishing was a contest between man and fish. If the fisherman came up empty, he didn't eat. If the fish lost the battle, he was eaten. That seemed like a fair way to look at the sport of fly fishing. To Wes, it was a challenge and a joy just to participate in the contest even if he went home empty handed.

But now it is no longer vacation time. Wes is home for good. And it isn't too difficult to pick up where he left off; sort of. After his travels and his inspiring work in the nation's capital he is eager to put all that

110

he has learned to work. There is a new sense of purpose to his efforts that assures him on a daily basis that he has made the right decision and that he is really home to stay for good.

The first piece of business on his agenda is finding a place to live. He is too old, and too private, to live in his folk's home anymore. He finds a small house in a good neighborhood just north of Main Street that is in need of repair. The old man who had lived there had been admitted to an old-folk's home. He quickly checked out of the facility by the simple process of dying. The house is vacant and owned by the old man's daughter who had left Feltondale long ago. She is anxious to sell and not too particular about squeezing the last dollar out of the property. Wes buys it "well" as they say in the real estate business.

His new home is a Sear's Catalogue Craftsmen-style kit house. The Craftsman-style bungalows were wildly popular in the early 1900's but had, over the years, fallen into disfavor. Wes is thrilled to have one. He has always admired the Arts and Crafts movement and the Craftsman-style homes that came out of it. Wes decides that he will initiate a one-man revival, at least here in Feltondale.

Wes's little home has a typical Craftsman bungalow design with a small front porch surrounded by a half wall. The porch roof is supported by four tapered square columns. The front door is made of oak that unfortunately has been painted more than once.

111

The floor plan is typical of what was called the California bungalow. The first room you enter is the parlor and directly behind it is the dining room. The two rooms are separated by half walls on each side with similar support columns to the ones on the porch. The dining room has several built-in oak drawers and cabinets. The one on the left has a mirror in the niche above a glass-door built-in cabinet. On the right side there is a built-in oak buffet with a counter on top of it. Above the counter, at the rear of the niche, is a sliding serving door in place of the mirror on the other side. The little serving door opens to the kitchen which is located behind it. The oak cabinetry in the dining room has unfortunately been painted just like the front door. One of the home owners in the past sixty or so years was either lazy, or stupid, or both. You don't paint fine wood; ever.

In the center of the rear wall of the dining room is a doorway that opens into a long hall. Entering the hall, the small kitchen is on the right and the bath and a closet are on the left.

At the rear there are two bedrooms on either side of the home. Both have built-in closets and one is slightly larger and serves as the master bedroom. There is a glass-paned door off of the kitchen that leads to the side yard and the rear of the house.

At the rear of the house is a small concrete patio that is big enough for a couple of chairs and a table and, of course, a BBQ. There is a narrow but deep back yard with a one-car garage at the rear with its door facing the alley. The garage is stuffed with junk but appears to be serviceable. When it gets cleaned out there should be room for his new Scout and maybe enough space left over to make a small work bench and store some garden tools as well. As it turns out, the Scout will usually be parked in front of the house and the garage will remain clean but will be empty most of the time.

Wes thinks that the home is structurally sound and that all the repairs that are needed are significant but mostly cosmetic. Almost everything Wes needs he is sure he can find right here in town.

The first Saturday after the house is formally his, he pays a visit to Dill at the hardware store to begin the process of restoring the house.

To his surprise, there is a new fellow working at the store. He is about Wes's age and based on his responses to questions about what is needed to do the job, Wes judges that he seems to know what he's talking about when it comes to carpentry and the like.

"I'm glad to meet you and I'm glad you're here as well Chris. I know you can be a big help. Here's a list of what I think I want. But you know what would really be great, is if you could come over to the house and make an assessment of what all is really needed to restore the place. I'm just an amateur and I'm probably missing a bunch of things. I'd be happy to pay you for your time. How about it; does that fall into your job description?" Wes asks.

"Well, I guess it does. After all you're spending your hard earned dollars at this store. But I wouldn't charge extra for it. To my way of thinking, that's just part of the job," Chris replies with a smile. "How about meeting this afternoon at five? What's the address?" Chris asks.

Later that same evening when they have made a tentative list of what is needed for the restoration, Wes and Chris retire to Smiley's Tap Room to double check their list and discuss a future course of action over a cold beer.

"You know Chris; it seems to me that you know quite a bit about wood working. Would you be interested in taking on a part-time job helping me make my house livable and loveable? I need to do it as fast as possible because I'm going nuts living with my folks. I'm just too old to be comfortable there, and I think my folks feel the same way, although they never would let on. My room still has my high-school trophies in it and the twin bed I slept in as a boy has somehow shrunk over the years," Wes says and then continues without letting Chris get a word in edgewise.

"Let me tell you what I'm thinking about Chris and then see if you would be interested in helping me. What I want to do is to restore the house to what it looked like when it was first built. Did you know it was a kit house from Sears? Well it is. And it is a Craftsman-style house which was really in vogue back at the turn of the century.

Ever since I visited the Victoria and Albert Museum in London during my European adventure I have been a big fan of William Morris and the Arts and Crafts movement he helped found back in the mid 1800's. He was quite a renaissance man. He thought that the industrial revolution and mass production were destroying the beauty of how and why things are made. He thought we were losing pride in making and owning hand-crafted things. And he probably was right. He thought the whole Victorian scene was way over the top and in most cases just plain ugly. I know he was right about that.

Anyway, his Arts and Crafts movement came over here to the states around 1900 and a guy named Stickley started a magazine called *The Craftsman* that championed all of Morris's principles of organic design and hand-made stuff and the like. And that magazine spread the Arts and Crafts movement all over the country. Out of that, architects came up with what they called the Craftsman-style house.

In California, architects like Greene and Greene, Dryden, and Maybeck used these design principles in their buildings, large and small. The California bungalow was born but it was really just a West-Coast version of the Craftsman bungalow.

And there was furniture made to match this architecture called the Mission Style and Stickley had a lot to do with that. And Art Deco and Frank Lloyd Wright came out of that too.

Anyway, what I want to do is completely restore my house back to what it looked like before a succession of unenlightened owners painted all of the beautiful oak woodwork and really took the soul right out of the place.

So, what do you say; can you find the time to give me a hand? How are you with working with wood?" Wes asks.

"Well Wes, I've always loved to work with wood but I have to warn you that a project like this will take some time," Chris replies as he takes a long sip of his beer. "To do it right you can't rush it. Especially removing paint and restoring wood; that's a long and tedious process that requires patience and perseverance," Chris pauses and sips his beer again and appears to be thinking Wes's proposition over. He finally continues.

"I think I can accommodate you but I'll have to check my social calendar. If there are any conflicts, I'm sure I can shuffle things around to help you get your place restored. I've got the time and can always use extra money, but I'd like to be part of this for a couple of other reasons. I'm anxious to learn about this Arts and Crafts movement and what your bungalow will look like when it's all spruced up. And I sure don't want to be in any way responsible for you going off the deep end by sleeping in too small a bed. I know how that can drive a man crazy."

"That's great Chris. I know we'll have fun doing this," Wes replies.

"So Wes, do you want to start tomorrow early? I've got the keys to the hardware store so we can pick up enough to get started without being disturbed. Dill doesn't work on Sundays but he's never said I couldn't."

"You've got a deal Chris. I'll pick up some donuts and coffee and meet you in front of the store at eight."

Wes's house is ready in two months by the long hours of moonlighting put in by Wes and Chris. They complement each other well and work together in a natural rhythm. They seem to anticipate each other's actions and needs which speeds up the work. And like Wes thought, the job is fun; more like a succession of rewarding accomplishments, than a tedious bunch of undesirable chores that they are compelled to get through. And the result is much more remarkable than they had anticipated. They've really done the old gal proud. She could be a model in the new Sears catalog if they still sold mail order houses. The Craftsman revival in Feltondale has begun; although nobody but Wes and Chris know it yet.

All the furnishings that were left in the house are past their days of being useful and are destined for the city dump. Chris and Wes scrounge a few second-hand items of furniture to get the home livable. Wes splurges on a new bed and linens and the two friends have an impromptu house warming with a six-pack of Molson and two large T-bones from the butcher prepared on Wes's new BBQ grill from Feltondale Hardware.

So begins a friendship that will last a lifetime.

Getting up to speed at the office is another matter. Wes hasn't really worked on a full-time, day-to-day basis with his father in years. The first thing he notices upon his return to the practice is how much it seems that his father has slowed down. It's either that his dad has always been someone who operates at an easy lope, and Wes doesn't remember it, or that, after the bustle of the eager beavers in Washington, D.C. his dad's stride suffers by comparison. After a week or so Wes figures out it is a combination of both. His dad is a little slower; and Wes is a little faster. He comes into sync by slowing down to a pace that is more in keeping with small-town Montana.

After all, what they are doing in their practice is not earth-shaking and it demands much more thoroughness than speed. Unless somebody actually dies in the interim, a will doesn't need to be done in a flash. The clients don't expect it or appreciate it, and if you are too quick with your results they figure you haven't worked hard enough or long enough to warrant what they always think is such an outrageous fee. If you could sell legal advice like beef, by the pound, it would be a lot easier all around.

Wes can't believe how good it is to be back at work. It seems to him that his father is almost to the point that he might want to retire. All the while Wes has been away his father has had to handle the practice by himself and it appears to have taken its toll. Wes realizes that he must take on the lion's share of the work and let his dad gracefully step aside when the time comes.

But Wes has other plans outside of the practice that will require a lot of his time so he needs to get up to speed quickly so he can squeeze them in. But he has to be careful. He needs to work a bit faster but not give the appearance of doing so, so his clients and his father don't notice and take umbrage. Nobody likes a smart aleck.

He learned a lot working for the Congressman in Washington, D.C. One thing he figured out was that government, local, state, or federal, operates best when it creates opportunity in the private sector and then gets the hell out of the way. The old adage that an enterprise run by the government has the compassion of the IRS and the efficiency of the Post Office is not far off the mark. Wes wants to apply what he has learned in Washington, D.C., both positive and negative, to solving the problems of the town that bears his name.

One way he sees he can best accomplish this goal is to run for the city council. He has observed in his work with Weaver that he is not destined to be some sort of Machiavellian power behind the throne.

He should be able to win a council seat in his own right. He figures he is personally well enough known and certainly he has name recognition. He just needs to put forth some ideas that will help his town to grow without losing sight of what makes it a livable and enjoyable small town.

He figures he should run the next time a seat opens up. He doesn't want to alienate any of the incumbents by challenging them and it shouldn't be too long a wait. There are a couple of the councilmen who seem to have been in office since before Montana became a state. Somebody has to retire soon or at least die.

So he'll bide his time. And that's a smart move. He's been away for so long that he might be seen in some quarters as a carpet bagger even though he's about as far away from the Deep South as you can get and still be in the United States. Patience is what is needed and he can fill the time by outlining some ways that he can improve the economic outlook of the town.

He can also initiate some other important projects; like teaching Chris how to fly fish.

CHAPTER TWELVE ... 1963, MONTANA

Chris is precariously perched on the next-to-the- highest rung of a very tall ladder. It's time to move all the hibernating garden tools from their top-shelf cave down to a more visible display he has created near the front door. Spring is coming and he thinks an assortment of secateurs, hose nozzles, trowels, and weeding forks, next to the Burpee seed stand, will remind the customers that it's time to get digging.

Attempting to wrestle a bunch of reluctant gardening tools into a burlap bag so he can transport them safely to their new home, he doesn't hear the bell on the front door ring as a new customer enters the store.

It is a young lady dressed in very fashionable clothes including a jaunty cap atop her upswept hairdo. Tres chic, especially for Feltondale where most fashion statements sprout from a basic garment created in the salons of Levi Strauss.

"Can anyone tell me if the owner of this wonderful establishment is around?" her words ring out in the empty store. Chris is startled and nearly loses his precarious footing. In the process his bag of tools falls to the floor with a loud crash and disgorges its contents at the feet of the lovely visitor.

"Oh my God, Miss, I am so sorry," Chris exclaims as he gingerly makes his way down the ladder.

"It's entirely my fault, Sir," she replies in an apologetic voice, a smile on her face. "If I had just looked up, I would have noticed you and I wouldn't have startled you when I could plainly see that you had your hands full."

"Well, if truth be known, Ma'am, I shouldn't have been up there when I'm alone in the store. And I'm a little afraid of heights which doesn't help my agility any when I'm high on a ladder, or anything else for that matter," Chris says as he climbs the rest of the way down from his perch to the shiny hardwood floor.

As if summoned by an inner call, both Chris and the young lady stoop down to pick up the array of garden tools on the floor. They arise from the chore in unison as well, but with less successful results. They bump heads and the tools clatter to the floor again. They could be in a 1930's screw-ball comedy. Capra would be proud of them.

"It seems to me that we'd best leave them where they are for the time being. Let's catch our breath and regain our composure," Chris laughingly offers as he gently pushes the errant tools into a neat pile with his booted foot.

"In answer to your question Miss, the owner, Mr. Dill Staunton, is down at Julia's Café having the blue-plate special for lunch. I can have young William, who's out back, fetch him for you if it's important. Or,

122

he should be back in few minutes if you care to wait. There's a chair next to the counter over there where the wives wait while their husbands are shopping; or vice versa."

"Don't bother William, I'm sure he's busy. I can wait," the young lady replies. "It does seem that I'm in the way but I assure you it is not my intent. Perhaps as you suggest I will wait over there by the counter before I cause any more commotion," she says with a smile.

With that she moves away and Chris continues picking up the garden tools. He feels her gaze on him and tries hard to be both nonchalant and as careful as possible while completing his task. He doesn't want to appear any more foolish than he already has. He has never been relaxed around the fairer sex and this beautiful young woman is no exception.

"You must be Chris, I've heard so much about you I feel as if I know you already. You've been here a while haven't you?" the young lady asks from her seat near the counter.

"I've been working here going on about nine months, Miss, but I don't remember seeing you in the store before," Chris replies. "Your right, by the way, my name is Chris" he continues, but before they can properly complete their introduction, Dill comes through the front door a tooth pick in his mouth. Chris is amazed at the surprised look on Dill's face; his eyes as big as blue-plate platters. A broad grin spreads across his face.

"Penny, my God, where have you come from? I can't believe you're here!" Dill yells.

"Yes Father, I'm home," she replies and father and daughter fall into each other's arms.

"Girl, you are a sight for sore eyes. I really mean it. Just look at you all dressed up in your New York finery. I can't believe you are actually here. I was just telling Chris the other day how it was just about time for you to pay a visit; and here you are," Dill rambles as he holds his daughter at arm's length. "Oh Dear, where are my manners, have you met Chris?"

Penny laughs, "Well, we weren't formally introduced but we sure met; literally. It's nice to meet you Chris. My dad has written about your exploits in rearranging the store and making everything work more smoothly. I hope you continue with that process. Dad's kind of stuck in his ways and I am certainly not the one to change him anymore. So it's all up to you."

"I don't mean to make a lot of wholesale changes here just embellish on things a bit," Chris modestly replies still reluctant to accept compliments with grace.

"He's done a lot more than that," Dill interjects. "We made up a little story about Chris being my cousin from Utah. Folks had no reason to not believe the story, so they did. That way Chris was accepted right off and he gets along great with all the customers. Besides your Aunt, Chris, and me, you're

124

the only one who knows about our little subterfuge. Even Wes doesn't know. So mum's the word. Okay?"

"Sure Dad, I don't want folks to think my Dad is a fibber; my lips are sealed", Penny responds.

"Now, how long are you going to be able to stay this time?" Dill asks of his daughter as he leans against the counter still in a slight case of shock.

"Well that's just it Dad. When I say I'm home I mean *I'm home*. I've left New York for good. I wasn't completely sure about my decision driving across the country but standing in these familiar surroundings with you, I realize I made the right choice in coming home. I'm in exactly the right place."

"I can't believe it. That's wonderful Penny. The best news this old man can imagine. Martha will be tickled pink. And your room is still the way you left it. The house has sure been lonely with you not in it. And there's still plenty to do around here; isn't there Chris?"

"Yup, spot on Dill, we've hardly made a dent in the ol' place," Chris replies. He has picked up some of the colorful local vernacular that ranges from the clipped speech of the cowboy, and the Queen's English from the Angus breeders that emigrated from the British Isles, to the peculiar idioms from the Deep South. In small-town Montana they all sound as natural as if they were born here especially when they are mixed together in the same sentence.

"Well that's nice work for you two," Penny comments, "but I'm only going to work here part time and only until I find something else to do; something more suited to that fancy education you paid for and all the things I've learned in the big city. There must be something I can do here in town that will put all the stuff I have stored in my head to good use. I might teach. Or work in the library, or something that I haven't even thought of yet. The field is fairly limited here so I might just have to dream up my own job and hire myself to do it. But I'll be happy to help you and Chris until I figure out what to do with my life. Okay Dad?" Penny asks.

"Sounds good to me honey, I'm just glad you're home," he replies still astonished at his good fortune. His daughter is back to stay.

Chris, who has been standing uncomfortably to the side, slightly embarrassed to be part of this somewhat intimate conversation, steps forward and offers a suggestion.

"Why don't you take the rest of the day off Dill and take Penny home and get up to date. You must have a million things to talk about. I can handle everything here, you've trained me well. And I can always get ahold of you by phone if I need to. So go on and git."

So they git.

CHAPTER THIRTEEN... 1963, MONTANA

Chris is learning how to be happy. For once in a long while, he is allowing himself to have a bit of faith in what comes next; a ray of hope. And his first hope is that his checkered past doesn't find him and ruin his future. But he realizes that that is beyond his control. He has done everything he can to establish himself in his new life; to be more open and receptive to the good things it has to offer. The past will have to take care of itself.

The only thing that has occurred to interrupt his growing sense of well-being is that Wolf has disappeared. Chris came home one day from work to find the side-yard empty. There were no signs of a disturbance of any kind; just an empty yard. Chris called out for Wolf and dutifully searched the neighborhood. None of his neighbors had seen or heard anything. It was as if Wolf had just vanished into thin air. After several days of getting used to living in a Wolfless world Chris came to realize that Wolf's departure was a natural   progression of their relationship. It was as if his departure were inevitable. Wolf had come to him when he needed a friend and stayed with him until he was settled in his new life. And then he moved on. He missed Wolf but he was not devastated. He realized that Wolf's presence had been an important step in his transformation from loner to increasingly useful member of society. Wolf had returned to whatever life he led before he hooked up with Chris. Perhaps he really was more Wolf than dog. But their time together will always be remembered with both fondness and mystery.

Chris discovers that honest work is both satisfying and fun. Dill keeps telling him he is making a real difference in the daily operation of the hardware store; that his changes are making the store more attractive and accessible to the customers. Chris is beginning to believe that what Dill says is true. The folks seem friendlier and he feels that might be because he is making an effort to be more friendly as well.

The other thing that has really improved his personal circumstances immeasurably is his new friendship with Wes. He can't remember when he ever had a real friend. He has always been a loner living in a safe but restricting world of his own creation. Letting others into it has always been uncomfortable.

Yet he and Wes really seem to hit it off. And that is somewhat astounding to Chris as their backgrounds are so completely different. And yet their relationship of friendship and trust is based on the present not on the past.

And Penny; in what way does she fit into how he is feeling? She is the only female he has been able to converse with without becoming tongue tied and at a loss for words. She is just naturally open and he guesses that that makes him able to open up to her as well. But there will always be a need for him to keep his guard up; at least a little bit. But he is more comfortable around her than he ever thought he could be and that's a good feeling; one he has never experienced before.

Penny has taken to working part-time at the store and her presence is both very pleasant and at the same time completely disconcerting. Sometimes Chris looks up from a task and finds her staring at him and then quickly turning away. But when he thinks about it, he does exactly the same thing. Are they engaging in a form of non-verbal flirting? Having had little experience in this sort of thing in his life, he can't really say for sure. But each time they have a chance to talk he becomes surer of himself and more comfortable with her. He is happy that she has that sort of effect on him and looks forward to their increasingly more-frequent exchanges with calm but eager anticipation.

Chris thinks again about the three of them. First, there is Penny. He knows she is happy to be back in Feltondale after her long absence. She seems to be looking for a fresh start here. And Wes? He came back here looking for a new start too. And Chris? He has found a home and a new life here as well. The three of them seem to be running to, or back to, something. And for all three of them that something turns out to be this little town in Montana. Maybe they'll discover that they're all looking for the same thing; and they'll find it together. Stranger things have happened.

Working with Wes on his house has reminded Chris of how much he loves crafting things out of wood; especially furniture. He has worked in several furniture shops in various parts of the country and he has always enjoyed the experience. Working with tools and making things; he has been enthralled with both the mental and physical process of creating furniture from scratch.

This realization has rekindled an idea that has been at the back of his mind. What if he could find a way to build furniture in Feltondale? Not in place of his work at the hardware store, but in addition to it. Maybe Wes could give him some advice on whether this is a reasonable thing to consider, and what steps he could take to make it come to fruition.

The next time he and Wes stop by Smiley's for a beer after work he broaches the subject. His new-found ability to verbalize his ideas is satisfying. His thoughts somehow flesh themselves out as he goes along and he finds himself talking a blue streak; as if the words just need to get said.

"You know Wes, this new, old, house of yours; it's a gem but since we finished remodeling it I've been reading some on the furniture end of the Arts and Crafts movement, Stickley and those guys, and your place really needs some new furniture to make it a true Craftsman house. I've made some furniture in my day; especially wooden pieces. And hand-crafted Mission style furniture in your home would really finish off all we started with the restoration work. If you're interested in the slightest bit, we could figure what kind of furniture you would like and I could sketch out my ideas. You'll need a dining room table and chairs, and for the living room, a sofa and loveseat, and some end tables and a coffee table. We could match the oak cabinetry in the dining room that we rescued from the layers of paint. How does that all strike you? What do you think?"

"Go ahead Chris, don't stop now, I'm sure as hell interested. I would love some new custom Mission style furniture. It really would complete the place, wouldn't it? So, how would you do this? And how can I help?" Wes sits back and encourages him to continue.

"Well I've been thinking for days of how to pull this thing off. I know one thing; I can't do it alone. It's too big a challenge. I'd need your help and probably Dill's as well. You see he owns this empty building across the alley back of the hardware-store annex. That would give me plenty of room to work. So if we can get that, we have a place to set up shop.

And, speaking of the annex, I've been looking into the idea of cutting a connecting door into the hardware store and using the space in the front part of that annex building for a showroom for wood stoves and heaters and the like. There's a good market here what with the harsh winters in these parts and the availability of cheap wood. We have stoves in the hardware store but they are in the back and nobody ever sees them.

Anyway, when I was scoping out the annex with an eye to this stove project, I went into the back storeroom and discovered a gold mine. Under some tarps I found an old wood lathe, a joiner, and a planer. They are high-quality tools and they surely cost a pretty penny in their day. And they are in good shape, so I guess you would say that their day is still here. They look as though it wouldn't take much to get them up and running and they'd be better than anything they make nowadays," Chris carries on.

"So let's say we've got a place for a shop and the major tools to go in it. The rest of the tools I would need we have at the store. Or we can get them. The only thing that is missing is the money to get the place up and running and to get the materials to build your stuff. Oak is not cheap, but it's not that expensive either. It's somewhere in the middle-range of the furniture grade woods that are available," Chris pauses and takes a sip of his now warm beer and momentarily changes the subject.

"If this is the way the Brits drink beer then I can see why they're so reserved. It takes all the fun out of it," Chris observes. Wes agrees with a nod and takes the opportunity to change the subject back and interject some of his ideas into the discussion.

"You've really thought this furniture thing through haven't you Chris. And I'm following you every step of the way. So we're on the same page as far as the style goes and the idea behind it as well. And you know, if you expand on it a little, your project sort of fits into what I have envisioned doing in Feltondale to make the town more self-sufficient. Maybe I could be part of the equation. If Dill provides the land, and you provide the labor and the entrepreneurial leadership, then that leaves me to provide the capital if we are going to have the four factors of production from Economics 101. So I guess what I'm saying is that I'd like to invest in your project and help it get off the ground. It might be good for Feltondale to have a custom-furniture manufacturer in town; so count me in. We'll start it out as a project to get me some furniture and see where it leads. Who knows it might take off. So, where do we go from here?"

"I tell you where we go from here. Let's go look at that building I talked about before it gets dark," Chris answers and they leave their warm glasses of suds sitting on the table.

After looking through the grimy windows of the building behind the hardware store they make plans to meet at the store entrance at seven in the morning. They'll see what Dill thinks of this plan they are hatching.

Wes and Chris meet in the morning and go to the coffee shop and waylay Dill. By seven fifteen he is on board. He promises to call the electric company to

133

turn on the power to the building in the alley and gives Chris the keys and the rest of the day off to clean up the place and move the tools from the annex across the alley to their new home; with William's help of course.

Wes promises to stop by at noon to help them move the heavy stuff and see if Chris has figured out what all this is going to cost and how their new company should be set up. He also is anxious to see what Chris has in mind for his furniture. Wes had stopped at the library last night on his way home and checked out a book on Mission Style Furniture and one on the designs of the Arts and Crafts movement. He sees from the cards attached to the inside front covers that these are the same books Chris checked out and are how he became so well versed on this subject.

Wes likes what he sees in the books, especially the part about the California Bungalows. They look a lot like his house and the interior pictures give an inkling of what it will look like with compatible furniture. He falls asleep thinking that it all seems doable and could be a successful enterprise. He is sure that Dill and Chris agree.

The Feltondale Furniture Company is born.

CHAPTER FOURTEEN ... 1963, THE PACIFIC

"Well boys, what do we have here?" asks the Captain as he breaks into a gale of laughter that is almost terminal.

"You call this a still?" he asks, regaining a modicum of composure.

"It's no better than a tea kettle with a copper corkscrew sticking out of the top. What did you think you were going to make with this Mickey Mouse rig; a pint a day? You've got to be kidding," the Captain is incredulous as he surveys the still the brothers and Manny have created.

"I was concerned when the First Mate brought you up to see me. My first thought was that you wanted to get the crew half sloshed and put a screeching halt to their ability to do what little work they do anyway. Then I thought you were on your way to starting some sort of illegal business right under my nose. But you haven't made enough booze to get the ship's rats tipsy." The Captain pauses for a breath as the three men before him began to realize that he is no longer mad at them for making moonshine in the first place, but rather that he's unhappy that they didn't make enough of it. They eagerly wait for him to continue, with a small hope that this debacle may actually turn to their advantage.

"I've got to hand it to you boys; you sure have discovered the secret to making good home-made hooch. You are alcohol artists of the first caliber. And, I bet if you put your mind to it, you could make a hell of a great bottle of rum. The problem is, you'll never make enough of anything with this contraption and what supplies you can steal from the ship's stores. To earn some serious money, you've got to think bigger."

John thinks he might explain that this was just a small test run and they had plans to expand but, for once, he decides to keep his mouth shut and let the Captain finish before he adds his two cents worth; so he just says "Yes Captain, you're right" then clams up and continues to examine the floor.

"Well boys," the Captain continues, "if you want to turn this into a business, what you need is a partner; someone who has the wherewithal and the gumption to furnish you with good equipment and allow you to distill large quantities of high-grade hooch. And you need raw materials and a distribution system. All of that is beyond your reach if you act by yourselves. If you take advantage of all that this fine ship has to offer, then we'll all succeed beyond your wildest dreams. Now, I just might make it my business to give you a hand; and for only a small portion of the profits. With your expertise and my financial backing and business acumen, we could turn this ship into a distillery-at-sea and deliver bath tubs of booze all across the Pacific and even beyond."

136

"Well Captain, we were just experimenting with what we had to work with," Charles finally responds. "We were just making enough stuff for our own amazement. Sorry we didn't offer to share but we didn't think you'd approve of our little venture. And what is it that you are thinkin' about anyway? Do you want to turn this ship into a floating still? That's what it sort of sounds like."

"I've got to be honest with you boys; it's harder and harder to make a living hauling stuff around the ocean for nickels and dimes. We are at the mercy of all sorts of things that we have no control over. Now, if we had a nice little business on board to augment the meager amounts we make with our freight operations, we'd be in a better position not to just survive but actually thrive. So what I'm proposing, as you say, is this. You provide the expertise and the labor and the good ship *Stella*, under my able direction, will provide the rest. We'll make ourselves some seriously fine booze and sell it at every port we go to, through our network of hungry and morally flexible port agents. This should generate a nice piece of change for our efforts. We'll split the profits, say, sixty forty, sixty for me and the ship, and forty for you lads. How does that appeal to you boys? Once again, don't let me rush you. You've got sixty seconds to think it over."

"Jeeze Captain, you've done it again," Charles says at the end of a minute of careful thought. "We might not like it that we're getting the short end of the split, but I guess we'd be idiots to turn it down. You've got most of the cards, but we at least are the ones who know how to make a good product. I guess we'll sign up for your program, but we'll need more help to run the kitchen and the still at the same time. We aren't magicians."

The Captain agrees with a smile and a nod. "When we get to Fiji we'll get some molasses and empty containers of some sort and whatever else that you think we'll need. In the meantime, let's employ the good offices of the Chief Engineer and the Bo'sun in building a still that will be able to make us all as rich as we need to be."

And so the *Stella del Sud* becomes the *Stilla del Sud* that changes the lives of everyone involved as they sail on a circuitous but inevitable, course to the production of vast quantities of liquid prosperity.

CHAPTER FIFTEEN ... 1963, MONTANA

It is a fine spring day. Winter has finally picked up its agenda and adjourned. It is warm in the sun and cool in the shade.

Wes enters the hardware store looking for Chris to thank him again for the job he did creating the magnificent dining room table for his new old home. He is surprised to find an attractive young lady behind the counter dressed in what seems to Wes to be a very fashionable outfit; especially for Feltondale and most certainly for a hardware store.

Somewhat taken aback he haltingly inquires about Chris and is informed that he is over at the furniture shop back in the alley.

"Are you new here?" Wes asks.

"Not really", she replies. "I used to work here in the past, but I've been gone for a few years. I got back in town a while ago."

"I see", replies Wes not really "seeing" at all.

"You don't recognize me do you?" Penny asks. "I certainly recognize you. You're Wes Felton third-generation member of Feltondale's first family and the current son in Felton and Son, Attorneys at Law."

Wes has a blank look on his face and then the light of recognition finally switches on.

"My God, you're Penny, Dill's daughter. I remember you as a bookworm of sorts. Weren't you valedictorian of your class at the high school? Then you went away to college didn't you. You certainly grew up well. I'm pleased to re-meet you," Wes blurts out extending his hand across the counter.

"Are you back for good?' he asks. "I just got back myself last fall. I bet your dad is happy to have you back," Wes continues haltingly just putting one sentence in front of another in random fashion.

"I'm back in Feltondale for good as far as I know," Penny states. "I'm just filling in here at the store while I figure out what I want to do with the rest of my life. That's a daunting challenge but I'm making slow progress. I'm going to do an occasional editing job for the publishing house in New York where I used to work. Other than that I'll work here when I'm needed and generally get reacquainted with my home town. I hope to find some way to fit in here; employment wise that is."

"Well, welcome home Penny, perhaps we can get together and discuss the employment possibilities in our one-horse town."

"I'd like that Mr. Felton, and if you want to catch Chris before he scoots off to lunch then you better get over to the shop," she offers pointing to the rear of the hardware store in the general direction of the furniture shop.

"I'll do that; and for heaven sakes call me Wes, my dad's Mr. Felton, and come to think of it, so was my

140

grandfather. Remember, we have a date to get up to date."

Wes leaves through the front door of the hardware store, goes around the corner and down the side street to the alley. He enters the alley and walks down to the furniture shop. Careful not to startle the occupant he waits until there is no machinery noise then enters the building. The room is one huge shop. The three big pieces of machinery that Chris had discovered are now in place and have been oiled and polished and are fully operational. In addition to the "classic collection" as Chris calls the formidable old tools, there is a bright yellow De Walt table saw and a miter saw as well on moveable stands. Chris has built plywood and two-by-four tables along one entire wall from front to back. There are other similarly fabricated working tables on wheels to use for assembly and gluing. There is a complete set of hand tools hanging on the wall. Wes is not sure of the use of some of these tools but knows that Chris considers them essential to the manufacture of custom furniture.

Wes counts six oak dining chairs with vertical oak dowels serving as the backs. They are in various states of construction.

"Here are the chairs for your dining room table. I should have them assembled and stained in two or three days," Chris says as he slowly looks up and smiles with a sense of accomplishment. "Dill sent me over here to work when Penny came in to manage the counter so I'm making real progress. By the way, I'm making a sign out of marine plywood on my scroll saw. It will spell out 'Feltondale Furniture'. I'll hang it out front so we'll be sure to get the attention of all the folks walking down this alley looking for custom furniture," Chris pauses and smiles. He looks around the room and then continues.

"Seriously Wes, what are we going to do with this fancy shop when I'm done with all of your furniture? You don't want to buy a bigger house do you?"

"God no Chris, but I tell you, it looks like this shop and you are already an integral part of Feltondale's future. Remember when I told you about my plans when we first had a few beers over at Smiley's? One of the reasons I came home was to apply what I had observed in Europe and what I learned in Washington, D.C. And what I had figured out was this; to be able to succeed as a nation or a town you need to be economically viable. You need to provide jobs. And I guess this place here is the first step in that process for Feltondale, and not just a place for me to get furniture on the cheap," Wes quips and embellishes on his ideas of the future of the shop.

"This enterprise Chris, Feltondale Furniture, is going to be a success; partly because of you and your talents and partly because Dill and I had faith in you and invested the money and land. What we need to do now is to make sure your talents are exposed to as wide a market as possible. That starts right here at home in this town. Get ready to be busy because I'll be busy letting people know you exist and what great furniture you create. If we are right about your talent, and we are, you'll make this company become a big success. That will generate tax revenues for the town, for the schools, and for the library and such, and will perhaps provide a few jobs for our young folk who would like to stay in this town and need a job to do so. It's as easy as that."

As Wes turns to leave, he has a second thought. "You've been working too hard Chris and you've accomplished a miracle in a very short time. Let's take tomorrow off. I'll pick you up right here at six o'clock. I want to introduce you to some fish."

True to his word, Wes picks up Chris in front of the furniture shop in the light of the false dawn just before the sun comes up. Both men wear heavy coats to fight off the chill. Wes assures Chris that it will be much warmer by the time they reach the stretch of the river under Mitchell's bridge. Wes is driving the tan, nearly new, International Scout he bought in the fall of his return to Feltondale.

They park the Scout just past the bridge and Wes unloads quite a lot of equipment and begins sorting it out. Chris has never been fishing in his life; but he supposes he is up for it. He has never liked being in water much, but Wes has extolled the virtues of fly fishing so many times that Chris is almost forced to give in. And here they are.

The sun is much warmer now and the scene is indeed idyllic. The river is shallow and wide with grassy banks. The slow-moving waters create only a few small ripples as they edge around the large rocks that appear to have been randomly tossed into the river by some ancient giant.

"Here's what you wear to keep dry as we wander up and down the river looking for likely spots to catch fish," Wes says as he hands Chris a pair of extra-large waders.

"Take off your jacket 'cause it's going to be hot. Put the waders on right over your clothes and put the straps over your shoulders and tighten them up. You want them snug so they'll be easier to maneuver in. The boots attached to the end of each leg should be large enough to go over your own boots. I hope they are snug enough too. It's rather hard walking in the river because the bottom is somewhat uneven. So be careful where you step. Don't fall into any large holes, not because you'll drown, but because that's where the fish hide and you'll scare the hell out of them."

Chris dons the waders and they seem to fit perfectly. He then gets his first lesson in how to use a fly rod.

"It's all in the wrist, Chris, just flick the line out in front of you. The idea is to make the fly land somewhere near to where you want it to. It should gently land on the water and float along the surface. Hopefully, the fish will be hungry and snap up the fly, hook and all. But don't let them catch you off guard. Sometimes when they lunge at the fly they can startle the dickens out of you.

144

If you get a fish on your hook, slowly draw him up near to you where you can get your net under him. Don't jerk him, or drag him too fast; you can pull the hook out. Just slowly lead him to you. When he comes toward you, pull back on the line and take up the slack. You'll catch on; it's easy."

Chris practices a few times on the grass and after a while he seems to be able to control where the fly lands pretty well.

"See there, I told you, you'd be a natural. Follow me now and we'll wade out and see if we can catch some dinner," Wes says as he gingerly steps into the slowly moving water.

They fish all morning moving up and down the river; Chris following in Wes's footsteps. They pass under the bridge and are working their way down stream when Chris decides to go over closer to the shore and explore an area under the branches of a willow tree that seems to have grown right out of the bank. He carefully casts his fly into a spot under a large root that arches out into the river. The fly has not even hit the water when a flash of twisting color comes flying out of the water and grabs his fly in midair.

Chris is so startled that he instinctively steps back to get out of the way. He trips on some sunken object in the river and falls ungracefully backwards. Miraculously, he still has hold of the rod when he lands and he slowly rights himself and arises from the river dripping with moss, water, and embarrassment.

145

At the end of his rod the fish swims quietly and then suddenly lunges toward him. Chris remembers Wes's instructions and pulls gently on the line to take up the slack. The fish is soon well within the range of his net. He clumsily removes the net from the snap on his waders and eases it under the now quiet fish. With a yell, he yanks up the net and the fish is out of the water. Chris has caught his first fish.

As beginner's luck would have it, that is the only fish they catch that day. It is a beautiful rainbow trout large enough for a meal for one person.

Wes shows Chris how to clean the fish and they load up and head back to town. Wes has to stop at the market to get a steak for his donation to the meal. They fire up the grill on Wes's back porch and cook their Montana surf and turf feast over the hot coals. They split the steak and fish.

The fish was not the only thing hooked that day. Chris is bursting with pride at his accomplishment and is so enthusiastic about the prospect of a future filled with fishing, that he decides to outfit himself the next day with all that he needs to become an angler in his own right. He even buys supplies to make his own flies; which turns out to be almost as much fun as actually fishing.

Wes was right. Chris is a natural.

CHAPTER SIXTEEN ... 1963, MONTANA

It isn't too long before Wes collects Penny for their first date. They go to Luke's grill next to the hotel. There aren't a lot of fine-dining choices in Feltondale. In fact, this is the only one.

They're seated in the back in the best booth in the house. This isn't due to the perception that Wes is one of the town's leading citizens, or to the fact that his law offices are upstairs and he is a frequent customer to both the grill and the café, but more to the fact that he knows how important tipping is. Money really talks; especially in Feltondale where it's not so plentiful.

Wes and Penny have no real agenda for the evening. They just want a chance to get acquainted and bring each other up to date on their adventures over the last years. They display an easy familiarity with one another borne out of the fact that they had hardly known each other in the past and are therefore free of the baggage that could encumber or impede their conversation. Even though they had both lived in Feltondale all the years of their youth, they were from slightly different eras and social strata. So they have somewhat different takes on life in their small town. They discuss the years they have each spent out of Feltondale. The things that they have learned

in their self-inflicted exile have given them both a
natural sense of confidence and a proclivity for
engaging in meaningful discourse instead of idle
small talk. The weather is never mentioned once the
entire evening.

Penny finds Wes to be charming, interesting, and
well-informed. But most importantly, he is engaging.
He really listens; as if it were more important to him
to understand what she is saying than to concentrate
on a clever retort. If he were to spell out his first
impressions about her he would have to admit that he
feels exactly the same way. And so the evening
progresses nicely, as if they are old, instead of nearly
new, friends.

It is amazing to Wes how their stories are so
similar. First the disenchantment with their small
town, then adventure and success out there in the big
city, followed by the realization that with their newly-
gained, more worldly perspective, their home town
doesn't seem at all as bad as it had when they had
escaped from it those many years before. It hadn't
changed; they had.

Penny asks him to expand on his years abroad and
in Washington, D.C. He is able to impart a wealth of
knowledge about what he had been up to during his
sabbatical without seeming verbose or overwrought.

When it is her turn she tells him about how she felt
growing up in their small, sometimes claustrophobic,
town. And what is was like to attend college in a
bigger town. And then move to the biggest town in

the world, all the time managing to maintain her small-town perspective. She feels she has gained a wealth of knowledge but realizes that it is now thinly overlaid by a veneer of sophistication.

As they are saying good night at Penny's front door they both comment that it really seems strange how they are so similar in almost all respects; really kindred spirits. It would seem that they have quite a future ahead of them and they take the first step along those lines by making a date for lunch in the middle of the week.

While Wes is all charm and sophistication, Chris is quite another thing. Penny sees in him a man whose strong native intelligence masks an insecure nature and a more than slight unease about dealing with people. It is both baffling and disarming. But come to think of it, his naiveté and direct manner have a charm all their own; different than Wes's, but charming never the less.

It is as if the old saying were not in the least bit true. In the case of Chris, Penny notices that familiarity merely breeds more familiarity. A nice feeling but she has to be careful with him. She is aware that it is a weakness in some women, and men for that matter, to see a diamond in the rough and to try to mold it into something that they think is desirable. If they succeed, they only discover that the changes they have so carefully wrought have rendered their target uninteresting and tame. They have destroyed what made them interesting in the first place. It would seem that malleability is not a trait that one should seek in a potential friend or especially a mate. Best leave well enough alone Penny thinks. Chris is doing fine without her unasked-for help.

Working alongside Chris is an enjoyable experience for Penny. He seems to gain more of a quiet sort of confidence every time she sees him. It is as if he were continually being reborn right before her eyes. When he is working in the furniture shop she often finds that she misses him and seeks a reason to be with him. So she makes it a habit of making enough lunch for two, and to go over to the shop during the lunch break. If she didn't do this, Chris would probably go to Julia's Café or just skip lunch. She assures herself that her visits are really just a way to look after Chris's nutritional needs. Really?

Though she realizes that he could be characterized as quite a different sort of man than the ones she has sought out in the past, she finds herself strangely attracted to him. He is a challenge but she doesn't know why. Nor, when she thinks about it, does she really care. To make things even more disconcerting, one day, when she is looking over his shoulder at how carefully he is gluing a wooden joint; he slowly turns and kisses her. And not a slight peck, but a full-fledged lip-to-lip smooch. To confound her even more, when he is finished kissing her he gets a slight smile on his face and returns to his gluing job without a bit of fluster or a "thank you" or "excuse me".

She doesn't know whether to be upset or happy. She decides later that she will be happily upset. And not upset like mad, but really more like being made to "set up" and pay attention.

The differences between Wes and Chris are many but the results to her feminine receptivity are the same. They are both unsettling and desirable; each in their own way. Thank God she doesn't have to choose between them; at least not for a while.

CHAPTER SEVENTEEN ... 1963, MONTANA

While Penny is struggling with her conflicted feelings, Wes is putting the second phase of his plan for Feltondale into play.

The first phase was the almost accidental establishment of Feltondale Furniture. This just sort of happened and he really had little to do with it other than providing some money which he is sure to get back with interest.

The second phase of his plan is entirely of his own doing; from the start. He believes that the merchants and businesses of Feltondale should create a Chamber of Commerce to promote their, and the town's, welfare. To this end, he solicits the support of Dill and Chris his closest business associates. His office, of course, will become a member, and he is sure he can talk Luke's Grill, Julia's Cafe, the Feltondale Hotel, and Smiley's Tap Room into coming on board as they are all in his building. All he figures he has to do to attract members is to keep the dues to a minimum and the perceived benefits at a maximum. There's the drug store and the market; all the shops, and even the Flying "A" gas station. Every business in town would profit by such an association; except maybe The Cornell Mortuary. As long as people keep dying and you're the only funeral parlor in town you really don't need to promote your services. You just have to show up with that big black Pontiac hearse and do your job. But who knows they might just join out of a sense of civic pride. It can't hurt to ask.

So Wes makes his rounds, promising much and actually offering little. He gathers quite a large group of members and they agree to meet once a month at Luke's Grill to organize and promote the businesses of Feltondale. Each will pay for their own lunch and the minimal dues will merely cover the cost of stationery, envelopes and the like. They can use one of Wes's empty offices as a headquarters, and naturally, Wes is elected president of the Chamber unanimously.

There really isn't a cause for the Chamber to champion at the moment. Wes figures it is enough for him if the Chamber merely exists and is prepared to take action on some future project, or problem, quickly and decisively if the need should arise. It is sort of like a volunteer fire department; organized and ready to serve if and when they are needed. As a bonus, all this work organizing, cajoling, and actually running the Chamber won't be wasted when it is time to run for the town council.

Besides his extracurricular activities Wes is busy at the offices of Felton and Son, Attorneys at Law, as well. As if by some law of mathematics, Wes's dad decreases his workload in direct proportion to the increased work Wes takes on. Nate is slowly putting himself out of a job and in a way this is a shame. Wes and his dad have always been a team; at the office and in abiding with Wes's mother's almost complete indifference to the both of them.

Wes and his dad have always had an easy camaraderie. For all of his life, Wes has assumed that his dad was on his side and that he had his best interests at heart. And Wes's dad has always assumed that Wes has the ability to deal with anything that comes along in his life, and it happily has become a self-fulfilling prophecy. There is a lot of assuming by each of them. But assumptions, without communication, can be dangerously wrong.

But Nate's slowing down is more than just a sign of the approach of old age. He is unaware that his health is actually precarious and his very life is hanging in the balance. He is overweight, and constantly in a state of stress though it doesn't show. And he drinks way too much, too often, and for too long.

When he suffers chest pains after a large dinner at the Grill, which he attributes to heartburn, Nate collapses at his solitary table. When the waiter notices him he tries to awaken him and, being unable to do so, an ambulance is called and he is rushed to the hospital. The hospital tries to contact his wife and son but can't find either of them. Attempts to revive Nate Felton are futile and just before midnight he dies without ever regaining consciousness. He is alone.

Wes is devastated. His father was such a young man. Wes just assumed that he would always be there; another assumption. To Wes his dad was really the heart and soul of Felton and Son. Now, only the "and Son" is left.

What Wes really regrets is that he had never taken the time to really get to know his father. He can't remember if he had ever told him that he loved him; and vice versa. Wes had been so busy with his own life that he never really thought about his dad much at all. He didn't discuss his plans and dreams with his dad; only with Chris and Penny.

Wes realizes that what was really sad was that he and his dad were more like pals than father and son. At least that's the way Wes felt. Maybe his dad felt differently. Maybe he longed for a closer relationship with his son. Now Wes would never know. His Mother wouldn't have the answer. Sadly, there was no one left to ask.

Both Penny and Chris try to help Wes get through his grief, and after several months he seems to be recovering from his loss. But there is a part of him that will never allow him to forgive himself for not loving his dad more. This realization tempers his unbound enthusiasm with a touch of humility that makes him a better person. But getting to that point is painful, both to Wes and also to the ones closest to him.

Penny draws closer to Wes during his period of grief. She listens to his painful admissions of guilt and assures him that he is not in any way to blame for his father's death. The two of them spend a lot of time together in the months after Nate's death and she watches him slowly regain his confidence.

But then one night, when Wes is at his lowest ebb, something very disconcerting occurs; he suddenly asks Penny to marry him. It comes right out of the blue and neither one of them really can believe he has done it. But he has. And there it is. He assures her, and himself, that his feelings are genuine; he really does love her so why not act on them.

Penny is not so sure. She is much more rational at this point and though she has strong feelings for Wes as well, she is sure that this is not the time for either of them to make such a rash decision. So she tells him she will have to take some time to think it over. And he should too. They leave it at that and keep the proposal and its aftermath to themselves.

CHAPTER EIGHTEEN ... 1963, MONTANA

Penny and her father are at home. Aunt Martha is at bingo so they are alone. Penny has told him that Wes has asked her to marry him and that she is in a quandary considering the fact that she has strong feelings for Chris as well as Wes. They sit across from one another at the kitchen table and her father reveals a secret that will alter the course of her life.

"You know I've told you all about your mother before," he begins, "but bear with me as I tell you one more time. And please don't ask me anything until I finish. This is going to be hard for me and it's very important that I don't miss a thing," he says as he takes a deep breath, almost a sigh, and tells his remarkable tale.

"As I've told you, your mother had a quiet beauty. Nicole was so much like you it's scary. She had dark hair that she wore long most of the time. And almost black eyes. She was tall and what we used to call lithe. I guess you'd call that graceful nowadays. Anyway, I was attracted to your mother from the first time I laid eyes on her. She had been in town only a few days when I met her. She was a nurse at our little hospital in town. She actually wasn't just a nurse; she ran the place. Old Doc Harder spent most of his time at his office downtown. He had an agreement with your mother that if she needed him for something she could not handle then he would come right away. If she didn't need him, then he preferred to be left to his own devices. Of course, if he had admitted a patient to the hospital then he would visit regularly. The rest of the time he would stop by sporadically to check on things out of a sense of duty I suppose. But she ran the place, that's for sure," he says, pauses, and then slowly begins again.

"Your mother was French-Canadian and her folks had moved down to Maine when she was just three or four. Her parents were killed in an automobile accident when she was sixteen and her aunt from Montreal came down to live with her. Right after high school she entered nursing school. It had been her life-long dream and the money that came to her from her parents' small life-insurance policy paid her tuition and a little bit more.

She worked as a nurse in several hospitals on the East Coast and when her aunt died she returned to her home town and worked at the local hospital. One day, she noticed an advertisement that we, on the board of the hospital here in Feltondale, had placed in a nursing magazine. We were looking for a head nurse. She wrote a letter to us that started a chain of events which ended up with her selling her house and moving here to take the job we offered her.

Like you Penny, she was interested in two men here in Feltondale and I still thank my lucky stars that

I was one of them. We went out often and had an easy and enjoyable, if not mercurial relationship. I think what she liked about me most was my steady, predictable ways; and my sense of humor. I was comfortable and funny even in those days. What I liked about her was everything. I finally asked her to marry me just before Christmas as I remember. I knew that she was interested in someone besides me but I didn't know who the other man in her life was. She never spoke of him and I really didn't see how she had time to see anybody else. But she did.

She said that she'd give me an answer after Christmas so I waited; reluctantly. And then one day just after the New Year began she appeared at my house. I asked her in and she seemed distraught, like she had been crying.

It was then that I learned of her other beau and why he had been kept a secret. He was married. She had been attracted to his mildly flamboyant ways and devil-may-care attitude toward life. He told her he was in a loveless marriage and his wife had no interest in him except as a provider for her somewhat extravagant lifestyle.

Your mother was in tears when she told me that they had made love after a dinner where they both had had way too much to drink. She had been ashamed and disgusted as well. The next day she told him she was no longer interested in him and that their brief and untidy affair was over. And she kept her word. But then the fates stepped in; but in a good way as it turned out.

Her period was due a week after the ill-fated tryst debacle and it didn't appear. She had always been as regular as clockwork. She felt that she was most certainly pregnant. It turned out she was right. She was devastated and came directly to tell me. She felt it was her duty to explain that she had disgraced me and could never dishonor me by taking my hand in marriage.

You know Penny, you would have been proud of me. I was forceful, even dashing in my response to her plight. I told her that I loved her, and that I always would, and that what she had done was a just a mistake, a lapse in judgment, and I was not then, nor could I ever be, ashamed of her. And if she would have me, my offer of marriage was still very much on the table, and I would raise her child, when it arrived, as my own and never mention it again. If we hurried, I told her, no one would know the difference. We could say the baby was early and that was that. She fell into my arms and I knew that she was mine. We both cried.

We were married in three days at the court house in the county seat and the next eight months and thirteen days were the happiest I had ever known. And then you arrived Penny and I found a lifetime of happy days.

I know you aren't aware of any of this part of her story. I swore I would never tell you. It was best that

160

you had the most idealistic image of your mother. And I've kept my word. But something completely unexpected has come up that makes me break my pledge. I must tell you the truth now no matter how much it hurts.

I am the father that raised you and loves you. But your genetic father was the other man in your mother's life; my unknown rival if you will. He was never told about you. We deliberately kept it from him. He had no need or right to know. And now you'll see why I had to tell you before things got out of hand with you and Wes.

You see, you and Wes share a biological father; he is Nate Felton. Wes Felton is your half-brother. You are allowed to love him, but only as a brother, you may never marry him."

Penny is shocked and disheartened by her father's story. But in some ways, after she thinks about it, she is relieved. She no longer has to choose between Wes and Chris. And the strange compatibility that she and Wes shared is no longer a mystery. They were born to love each other and to have close ties, after all isn't that what most sisters and brothers feel; a strong sense of kinship.

One thing is clear. She has no choice but to tell Wes. She cannot marry him but she has no right to make him think that it is due to some shortcoming on his part. The truth, as painful as it seems at first, will indeed set them both free.

So Penny confronts Wes with the truth the next day. She makes him promise to keep the whole thing a secret. She thinks to herself that she is glad his father, their father, is dead so he won't have to be told. She tells Wes that he is to think of Dill as her real father, and she and Wes must remain close friends and look out for and protect each other. Considering their unique relationship that is only natural. But no one must ever know. No one. Ever. And that is the way it is to remain for as long as she lives.

"The similarity we have by being brother and sister confused us and led us toward each other. We loved without knowing why," Penny states, and Wes reluctantly agrees. She tries to comfort Wes by suggesting that what they really had wasn't romantic love. After a while, both of them almost believe it.

But Penny has conflicted feelings about the whole situation. She has lost a suitor, true, but she has gained a brother. She cannot broadcast the wonderful news as it must be kept secret to protect her mother's, and for that matter, her father's memory. But she can forge a brother-sister relationship that will last a lifetime. She also no longer has to deal with the dilemma involving the proposal and the mixed feelings she had about her two suitors.

Chris now has a clear path and he doesn't even know it. Penny has to think of a way to let Chris know that he should continue his courting, such as it is. She knows he will need some help in deciding he wants to marry her and she is perfectly willing to provide a gentle nudge from time to time. To get the romantic ball rolling she comes up with a clever and yet simple plan.

Going over to visit Chris one afternoon she tip-toes into the shop and finds Chris standing at his work bench with his back to her, seemingly lost in thought. He is staring out the small window that is located above the bench. She quietly sneaks up behind him and taps him on the shoulder. When he turns around with a startled look on his face she returns the kiss he stole not long before. He receives it with a mixture of surprise and pleasure and she hopes that this non-verbal permission to move to the next level of their relationship does its magic. It does.

As she walks out the door she says over her shoulder,
"Tag, you're it."

CHAPTER NINETEEN ... 1963, MONTANA

It is almost one year to the day since Chris came to live in Feltondale, when another stranger arrives who will also have a major impact on the lives of the Feltondale folk. He parks his light-green newer-model Ford station wagon in a spot directly in front of the Feltondale Hotel. He stands by the open front door of his car staring down Main Street toward the mountains to the south. He is a big man dressed in khaki from head to toe. He is wearing a safari jacket similar to the one Clark Gable wore in "Mogambo" but instead of loops for rifle bullets it has been designed for fishing with many oversized pockets and brass grommets attached. The stranger appears to be lost in thought. He has a face that is vaguely reminiscent of Ernest Hemmingway, and for that matter Mr. Gable himself. He has a mane of almost completely white hair, annoyingly bright-blue eyes, and a ruddy complexion. He sports a pencil-thin mustache a la William Powell in "The Thin Man". All in all, he is an imposing figure.

His reverie ends as he suddenly comes to his senses. After carefully locking his car, he purposefully strides into the hotel lobby.

The hotel manager is on duty behind the check-in counter. He always takes the day shift as is his prerogative as the senior member of the hotel staff. He looks up from the papers he is shuffling and addresses the man fast approaching his desk.

"Good afternoon, Sir. May I help you?" he says in a reverential manner that borders on the obsequies.

"Believe it or not, I have come here for a room. Will you be able to accommodate me?" the stranger asks in a deep and authoritative voice.

"You are in luck, Sir. We have one room left, however it is the Presidential Suite. It has, in addition to a large bedroom and bath, a lovely sitting room that overlooks the thoroughfare below. I must confess, however, that though it may be called the Presidential Suite it, in fact, has never been occupied by a president of any kind as far as I know. We did have a judge stay in it once, however, and he seemed to enjoy it," the manager replies.

"Well I admire your optimism in choosing that name for your suite. Better to be prepared for an impromptu Presidential visit than to have to scurry around at the last minute throwing something together. I'll take it. Now if you have someone who can help me with my things I'd be appreciative," the visitor states.

As if he were given a cue, a middle-aged man in a plaid shirt appears and addresses the new hotel guest.

"I'll take your bags up to your room and move your car into our private parking lot at the rear of the hotel where no one will bother it. May I have the keys?"

"Certainly, but I would like to ask you to bring me the fishing gear in the back seat first with the utmost of care as it is very precious to me. My satchel, however, is in the trunk and you can bring it up to my room when it is convenient for you," he states as he hands his keys to the rustic bell man.

After filling out the register, he asks the manager a question that seems more of a demand than a request.

"Who is the best fly fisherman you have in town?"

"Well that's easy," the manager replies. "If you had asked me that two years ago I would have said old Lee Chesnutt. He was the most experienced fisherman in these parts. However, he passed away and now I guess that young Wes Felton would be the heir to the angling throne. And as luck would have it, his offices are upstairs above the café next door. If you would like, I will carefully guard your fishing gear while you pay him a visit. As I said his name is Wes."

The stranger nods a thank you and leaves as he arrived; with vigor.

"There's a gentleman to see you Mr. Wes," Donna the office manager of Felton and Son announces into the intercom. In a few moments Wes steps out into the reception area and the visitor comes forward with outstretched hand.

"My name is Charlie Smith and I've been told you are the preeminent fly fisherman in these parts."

"My goodness," Wes replies. "I had no idea I had such a lofty reputation. But I do love to fish; how may I help you Mr. Smith?"

"I'm in the area looking for an ideal place to do some fly fishing. I was hoping you could give me the location of such a spot or, better yet, join me tomorrow for a day's fishing."

"Short of arguing a case in front of the Supreme Court I can't think of anything I would enjoy more tomorrow than fishing. Where are you staying Mr. Smith?" Wes asks.

"Please, call me Charlie. I'm just next door at the hotel and I'm going to make an early night of it so let's meet at six AM in front of the hotel if that's all right with you."

"That's fine Charlie. We can ride in my car; it knows the way by heart. And may I ask if we can bring along my best fishing buddy, Chris? He always brings luck in his tackle box."

"By all means, I'm sure we can use all the luck we can get. Expertise only goes so far. I'll get the café to pack us up a picnic for three and I'll meet you at six." And with that Charlie turns and leaves with a slight bow to Donna.

The morning breaks clear and crisp and the forecast promises a fine day for fishing. Wes and Chris roll up to the entrance of the hotel promptly at six to find Charlie waiting with all of his gear and a large cardboard box filled with food and drink including coffee for the trip to the river.

The day is perfect; and the fishing is as well. Chris and the luck in his tackle box have exceeded expectations. All three have their limits by four in the afternoon and settle down on the banks of the river. Charlie breaks out a flask of very good brandy and the three toast their good fortune.

Charlie says that he has a business that deals in travel and shows a real interest in the town and the area. Wes, and to a lesser extent Chris, fill him in on all that they can think of about the history and prospects for Feltondale. Wes speaks of his creation of a Chamber of Commerce and his dream of helping the town create a more viable economic base. And he tells Charlie about Mitchell and his father, and the struggles of the Clark Ranch; site of this great fishing spot.

Chris talks about starting Feltondale Furniture and his ongoing efforts to create authentic handmade furniture that is also affordable. He states that if he can make a bigger success of the shop he will be able to train some of the more gifted wood-shop students from the high school in the art of making furniture and show how they can actually earn a living doing it.

The afternoon passes quickly and Wes invites his companions over to his house to feast on fish. The evening is enjoyable with Charlie and Wes swapping fishing stories. It is well after midnight when Chris and Wes walk Charlie over to the hotel and say goodbye.

But they will meet again.

CHAPTER TWENTY ... 1964, THE PACIFIC

The *Stella del Sud* has plied her liquid cargo for almost a year now. The Captain and Chief Engineer, as promised, have created a miraculous distillery out of old engine parts and materials they have scrounged from various ports-of-call on their rambling itinerary.

A small boiler left over from the diesel conversion serves as a basic heat source. Several large covered vats are used to ferment the "wash". With two vats they can ferment two batches at the same time increasing their overall yield. The large-gauge copper coil is fitted into the still itself by the use of a connecting device concocted by the Chief Engineer. Large five-gallon glass containers with huge corks are obtained as well. They are used to house the final product, which is sold in bulk to various watering holes in ports across the Pacific as arranged by the ship's agents. Some of the more enterprising of these agents actually rebottle the spirits into smaller bottles, labeling them with romantic names and selling them to retail stores or directly to the public. They would have tried to do that right on the *Stella* but it was hard enough to keep a still running, let alone a bottling plant, on a ship that is continually bouncing up and down and all around. So they stick with wholesale sales. It's easier.

The quality of the *Stella's* product precedes them and soon they have a string of port agents eager to represent them and sell the fruits of their labor to the thirsty public.

The brothers usually use sugar cane juice and molasses for their "wash" and distill the fermented results into excellent-quality rums, both a light variety for cocktails, and a more lethal dark rum perfect for umbrella topped fruit drinks or just plain sipping. Their enterprise is a success and the profits make for a happy and, even somewhat loyal, crew.

For the first time in their lives, the brothers have a steady source of income and begin to pile up a considerable stash of cash. They invest some of the lucre in the purchase of new passports, social security cards, and driver's licenses in Hong Kong. They are expensive but are first rate from a master forger in the Crown Colony.

But there is something that could possibly impede their eventual return home to America and their beloved southern backwoods. Somehow, they have the insight to realize there is a problem, but not the mental acumen to come up with a solution. They know that a massive hoard of assorted bills from many different countries, will not serve them well as a means of exchange. It would be nigh on impossible to turn into dollars without raising flags. Too bad the proceeds from their various alcohol related sales are

always in the currency of the buyer. The Captain
cannot or will not run them through the ships
channels to exchange them into a single currency as
this would tip off the owners who are not taking part
in this little money-making endeavor and would be
most cross if they found out about it. The Captain's
offer of keeping the money for them is not an
acceptable alternative either as they do not trust the
lovable but wily leader in the slightest. The brothers
will just have to think of something.

Bangkok, the eastern terminus of most of their
voyages, is a favorite place of theirs. For some
unknown reason they have a great respect and affinity
for the Thai culture and the people; especially the
women. They probably wouldn't describe their
feelings in quite those words if they were ever asked,
but they love to roam around Bangkok and take in the
numerous sights, sounds, and smells of this
remarkable city. It is a far cry from the usually seedy
and more backwards sorts of ports they visit along
their less than rigid cargo and moonshine route. And
they know all about backwards.

One day, at the beginning of a three-day call in
Bangkok, the brothers stumble across a dicey situation
that evolves into a solution to their monetary liquidity
problem.

While heading back to the ship from a night on the
town where they had sampled generous portions of
exotic wine, women, and song, they come across a

171

disturbing sight. Two men are attempting to rob a smaller, older man of his briefcase. The men have knocked the old man to the ground and one of them is pulling on his briefcase. He hasn't noticed that the straps of the briefcase are wrapped around the wrist of the old man and that he is not only slowly retrieving the briefcase, but is also removing the old man's arm from its socket in the process. The other young man is standing to the side laughing; but not for long.

Never ones not to step into the fray without fully accessing the situation, the brothers quietly launch themselves at the attackers. The brothers first come up behind the laughing man, one on the left and one on the right. They pull back their arms like major league pitchers, let go, and hit him on either side of his head. He drops like a rock. They repeat the process with the other robber who is still pulling on the old man. They get the same result.

John helps the old man to his feet while Charles begins to drag the would-be robbers into the bushes at the side of the walkway. When they awaken, and their equilibrium returns, as well as their hearing, they will decide that there are strange forces at work here in this particular part of town. It would be best to stay away.

The little old man the brothers have rescued is most grateful and invites them to escort him to his home which is only one block from the scene of the crime. He politely asks them in for a spot of refreshment to celebrate his good luck occasioned by their appearance on the scene of his misfortune. The brothers accept and soon they are ushered into a large home surrounded by a high wall and a lovely garden. The vestibule is made of white marble and the walls are festooned with silk wall hangings of exquisite quality and design. Upon entering the large main sitting room, they are overwhelmed by the luxury of the furnishings and the plush yet exotic feel of the place. They are invited to sit while a servant, who has appeared out of nowhere, pours them each a large snifter of brandy.

The boys from Georgia believe they are being entertained by royalty; and in some ways they are. Their host, Mr. Wang, while diminutive in stature, is very large in wealth and power. He owns a prestigious wholesale gem business that deals in a variety of precious stones and has customers all over the globe.

"I am forever in your debt, gentlemen," Mr. Wang tells the brothers. "I was most careless in my choice of routes to my home. I should have never taken that shortcut through the alley way. I could have been badly injured or even killed and this would have been most unfortunate and ironic as I was only carrying papers in my briefcase; nothing of value except to me. Please tell me that there is some way in which I can reward you for your gallantry in driving off those villains," he says in perfect English without a trace of the sing-song flavor that many Asian speakers afflict upon the language. "How can I repay you for your valor? Perhaps an assortment of Thai currency would be in order?"

"That is not necessary, Sir" John answers. "It's not that we are not grateful for the offer but we have all kinds of funny money stashed on the ship we live and work on and we don't really know what to do with it all. You see, from time–to-time we earn a little extra money over-and-above our wages. But it really isn't of much value to us 'cause there is no way to change it into dollars out here without taking a big hit. It seems that dollars are really precious in the Pacific. And when we hit landfall for the last time and return to live in the USA it'll be almost impossible to deal with all of this foreign cash. It's going to be a real pain when it comes time to change all this funny money into good old American dollars. And all this money is real bulky to carry around so we have to hide it on the ship and we're running out of hiding places."

"Gentlemen, I think I understand your dilemma and perhaps our meeting was most fortuitous for both of us," Mr. Wang replies. "If I may, I would be honored to be of help in solving both your storage and liquidity predicament.

You see, I deal in precious gems all over the world and I can see how I can be of great service to you. I am in your debt for the rest of my life and I will be most honored to repay this debt by being your banker in a way. What I have in mind is this.

If you would like, I can change your various currencies into one type of currency on paper like the British Pound Sterling or the US Dollar and then you may purchase with the money a few valuable precious gems from my inventory; at wholesale of course. These will be easy for you to carry in a money belt around your waist where they will always be safe especially considering your size and your prowess with your fists. When you are ready to cash your gems in you may do so at any number of places in the world at the offices of my gem-broker associates who deal with me on a regular basis. I will give you a list of these reliable associates and a letter of introduction that you may use for this purpose and I assure that they will charge you no more than three percent to exchange the gems at face value into dollars or whatever currency you choose. How does this proposition seem to you? Remember, this is debt of honor and I must repay you for what you have done for me."

The brothers are a bit leery of dealing in gems as they know nothing about the process and could be taken advantage of without even knowing it. They could arrive back home someday with a bag full of finely-faceted colored glass. On the other hand, as Mr. Wang says, he thinks he owes his life to their intervention and these Orientals are a funny breed; they take honor very seriously.

The brothers decide to turn some of their cash into jewels and then take them to the next port and find a jeweler who can give them an idea of what they are worth. If Mr. Wang is on the up and up, then the next time they are in Bangkok they can trade the rest of their cash into gems and finally rest assured that they are not going to be robbed or cheated. Hell, if old Wang is serious about rewarding them who are they to disappoint him.

"I guess that that sounds real generous of you, Mr. Wang. We'll go back to the ship now and tomorrow we'll bring you over some of our money and you can change it into gems for us. We'll give it a try. Maybe you're right, your good fortune is ours too."

"Rest assured gentlemen, I owe you my life and I will treat our transactions now and in the future as a sacred trust; as if they are sanctioned by my gods. Meet me tomorrow at my place of business and I will give you a full accounting of your money according to the published prices of currencies in the daily paper. Then I will exchange that amount into an equal amount of precious stones. It is my duty," Mr. Wang promises as he proffers a business card and bids them goodnight.

With that the brothers return to the ship and fall into their bunks. In the morning they retrieve stacks of bills from their hiding places and go to the address on the business card Mr. Wang gave them.

They are greeted warmly and ushered into an inner showroom where they are seated at a large round table and their cash is counted out. Mr. Wang carefully does the math for them using the current exchange rates from the paper as promised. He actually gives them a stack of American dollars so they will not be confused and then he buys gems with the money. In addition, Mr. Wang presents them with two large leather money belts with small zip-up compartments perfect for carrying gems.

"I hope you gentlemen are more content with this method of carrying your treasure and here is a list of my world-wide associates and a letter from me that you can present to any of my associates in the world. As I said last night, they will exchange your jewels at full price less a customary three per cent fee. I can also assure that they will give a comparable wholesale price for your gems. All in all, it is a most agreeable arrangement for all of us. I know that at the end of our transactions when you are safely home in America you will look back and you will be most happy that you stopped to help an old man in his time of trouble."

In their next port of call, they take one of the red gems which Mr. Wang valued at seven hundred U.S. dollars to what they are told is a reputable jeweler. They ask for an appraisal. The result is that they have not been cheated. If anything, the gem is worth more than what they paid for it. They stow their letter of introduction and the list of associated dealers, along with their faultless ID's in their money belts alongside the gems.

The brothers continue their adventures across the southern and eastern oceans and when they are in

Bangkok they eagerly seek Mr. Wang and purchase new baubles to add to the collection they each carry safely tucked away under their sea-worthy denim shirts. They get a few appraised from time to time and they are not being cheated. They didn't think they were but, when you're dealing with money, it's always best to err on the side of caution.

Their money problems are solved. They will be able to go home some day and change these portable gems into dollars, go back to rural Georgia, and live like kings, or perhaps just princes. At least that's the plan for now.

CHAPTER TWENTY-ONE ... 1964, MONTANA

The firm of Felton and Son, Attorneys at Law, is once again on an even keel. Wes has survived the devastating period of grief when he had to mourn both the death of his father and the loss of his prospective bride. He finally feels like his old self again and continues the practice of law with renewed vigor. Hopefully in the future he will meet another woman who will capture his fancy. He will marry, and there will be a new son who will eventually join the firm to flesh out the "and Son" portion of the sign on the front door.

One blustery day in March, while Wes is deeply involved in a disputed will, Donna brings him an envelope that came in the morning mail addressed to his personal attention. It carries the crest of the Childon Hotels and she has not opened the envelope. Inside there is a letter addressed to Wesley Felton III, Esquire:

Dear Wes:

First of all, let me thank both you and Chris for a most delightful day of fishing and camaraderie. You may have wondered why I was so interested in your town and the Clark Ranch. The answer to that is that I love to fish.

You must forgive my subterfuge in using the name
Smith but I like to travel incognito. When people know who
I am they are always uneasy and it ruins any chance I have
to enjoy myself.

The purpose of this letter I'm sure will be of great
interest to you as a booster for Feltondale. As you may
know, my hotel chain also includes a number of specialized
hotels and lodges around the world.

I would like to build such a lodge near Feltondale on the
knoll right above where we fished on the Clark Ranch. I
would like to engage your services to that end. I need to
buy or lease the property in question and obtain an
easement for ingress and egress to the lodge and for access
to the river for the purposes of fishing.

It is my hope that I can build a small well-outfitted lodge
for a maximum of thirty fishing fans such as myself to
spend time, and money, in your area. If you are successful
in bringing the Clarks on board then I will send one of my
senior engineers to create a design of this lodge. Your and
Chris's input would be welcome.

It is my hope that this project will help the employment
opportunities for Feltondale that you so passionately spoke
of on the banks of that lovely river.

Please feel free to call or write me to further discuss this
project and be sure to give my best to Chris and assure him
that he will be building the furniture for this project.

Cordially yours,

Charles J. Childon aka Charlie "Smith"

Chairman of Board
Childon Hotels International

A new economic opportunity appears be coming to Feltondale. It seems Wes's constant promotion of his economic hopes, plans, and ideas seem to engender economic changes without any special planning, conniving or arm-twisting on his part.

Wes replies to Charlie's letter with enthusiasm and expresses a strong desire to be part of this venture.

After negotiating with Mitchell and his dad, and even conceding that the lodge will be named after them, "The Clark Lodge", he procures an outright purchase of several acres that include the spot which Charlie had designated to be his choice of where he wanted to locate the lodge. Along with the land Wes secures an easement in perpetuity for the road that leads to the lodge site, as well as for fishing rights on the entire length of the river located on the Clark Ranch.

The Childon engineer is a down-to-earth fellow who operates in an open manner and who welcomes input from the local folks. Wes and Chris are a great help to him in designing a lodge that will be organic, becoming part of the land and not just appurtenant to it. Frank Lloyd Wright would be proud of the results.

The lodge is comfortable and luxurious at the same time. In the center of the great room is a huge two-sided fireplace made of local river rock. It is a massive structure both imposing and welcoming. The lodge walls are fashioned from logs obtained locally and the entire structure is harmonious to its site and to the general locale.

The furniture is all made by Chris and the Feltondale Furniture Company and they become the premiere example of what will become the National Park Lodge Collection.

It takes over a year to build the lodge and from the start, it is a success due in large part to the fact that it is part of the Childon empire with all of its promotion and booking resources.

As a result of the success of the Clark Lodge, many other ranches in the area make their parts of the river available for fishing and the entire effort is coordinated by the Feltondale Chamber of Commerce. This includes the training and management of a select cadre of local guides to cater to the needs of the anglers who come to town to spend their time and their money.

Wes can see the fruits of his labors reaping benefits for his town. Will wonders never cease?

CHAPTER TWENTY-TWO ... 1965, MONTANA

Marge Clark, Mitchell's little sister has returned to the ranch on a well-earned and infrequent vacation. She is impressed with the fishing lodge and it's great to spend some time with her brother and dad. She hasn't been home in a long while. She likes to think that the trip is just for a visit with her family but she knows, not so down deep, that it is really motivated by a letter from her brother that said that Wes Felton is back in town and he is still single. After all the years he has been in her thoughts she figures that maybe it is time she should try to do something about that.

She had moved away from Feltondale when Wes had returned with his law degree. Before that, she had flirted with him when he first came back from the war but he didn't pay much attention to her because she was a kid and he was busy getting ready for his return to Yale. So when he left for Yale late in the summer she was only a little heart broken. She flirted with him again when he came back from Yale law with his degree in 1951 but he still didn't pay attention to her overtures. But this time it was different. They were older and their age difference didn't matter; but his lack of attention did. But it wasn't just her; it seemed that he didn't want to be in Feltondale at all; at least that was the way Marge saw it, and she saw it right. He had gotten away again. Maybe Wes was just unattainable.

So she decided she had to create a life for herself without him. And to do that, she had to move somewhere other than Feltondale. Maybe she should go to college she had thought? She had the grades from high school, and her dad had often told her she should go to college. So what was keeping her? Nothing.

She applied to several colleges and was accepted both at Colorado State and the University of Texas. She chose Texas. It was further away and she had heard that Austin was a great town. So late in the summer she moved to Texas and found that she rather liked it. In some ways it was similar to Montana, just flatter and hotter. But the folks in Texas had a similar attitude of self-reliance that made her feel at home. She loved the hustle and bustle of the student life as well.

After the first two years, when her counselor was eager for her to declare her major, she looked back on the courses she had taken so far and decided that the most interesting and useful subject she had taken was Economics 101. She hadn't the slightest clue why, except that it seemed to her that what she learned from that class had real relevance to modern-day life and would be a practical choice as a major. You could apply economics to almost any endeavor so she elected to become a business major with a minor in a newer field of study at the university; communications.

Her last two years were most satisfying. She really applied herself and graduated with honors in 1955.

Marge's father and brother made the trip from Montana for her graduation and were hoping that she would be coming home, but she wasn't ready to bury herself in Montana; at least not yet. She wanted to get out in the world and see what her new degree could bring her. There had to be a place for a smart, pleasant looking, young lady with a powerhouse degree. She decided her best bet for a good job would be in the Longhorn State where the University of Texas was revered and the cache of her degree would carry the most weight in the job market. So she went to Dallas and applied for a job at a local television station. Happily, she was offered a job as an assistant to the programming and production manager.

For the first year she was nothing but a glorified secretary. But she kept her eyes and ears open and tried to make herself invaluable. Her boss was Mr. Louis Grant. When she sees the Mary Tyler Moore Show for the first time the irony is not lost on her. Her Mr. Grant, however, was not a gruff and misogynistic boss but rather the opposite. He recognized Marge's talents and allowed her to progress from the position of accessory to the station operations to a full partnership in production and the acquisition of programming for the station. She stayed at the Dallas station for three years until Mr.

Grant was suddenly taken ill and had to retire. She was passed over by management and a man with less seniority and less talent got the job although Marge was sure that she was more qualified to fill Mr. Grant's shoes. She decided to take a look at what other opportunities were out there in her chosen field.

Not long after she began searching, she got wind of a position for a production manager at a television station out in west Texas in the small town of San Angelo. She took a trip into the west of the state to apply for the job in person. This action, plus her resume and a letter from her well-respected ex-boss Mr. Grant, got her the job. She found herself in charge of the programming in a town that reminded her of Feltondale; a dusty, dry, version but one with a similar sense of independence coupled with a positive community spirit.

The television station was an ABC affiliate and most of the prime-time programming and some of the daytime shows were acquired directly from the network and required little attention from her. There was, however, the rest of the air time to account for.

The acquisition and management of locally-produced shows demanded most of her time, talents, and resources. A "Dialing for Dollars" movie ran in the afternoon with a local host and many local sponsors that helped to fill the station's coffers. There was a local morning news show that was folksy and homespun; a sort of farm report with pictures. There was also a kid's show in the afternoon after the movie, hosted by a rather large and somewhat disheveled man dressed in railroad overalls and an engineer's cap who went by the moniker of "Engineer Phil". He had seen a similar show on a visit to Los Angeles and had liked it so much he took the entire format of the show and moved it to San Angelo. The TV market was so small there that no one from LA noticed, or if they did, they didn't care.

At the end of each show the kids got their glasses of milk and played "Red Light, Green Light" with Engineer Phil playing along.   He had an electric contraption that one supposed was from a railroad line but was in fact a modified city stop light. When the light was green you drank your milk. When it turned red you stopped. Easy? Sure. But not for Phil. He'd deliberately mess it up; drinking on the red light and stopping on the green. It was a simple game for kids that he muffed every day to howls of laughter across the county. He was a beloved institution around San Angelo and had a loyal following. And not just with kids.   There was a rumor running around that the day drinkers in the local bars just outside of the dry town used to play "Red Light, Green Light" along with Engineer Phil but with glasses of bourbon or beer instead of milk. They often muffed it too, but for different reasons.

Engineer Phil had his own production assistant, his wife, who did all of his actual production work so Marge had little involvement with the show with the exception of making sure that requests for Engineer

187

Phil to appear at birthday parties and store openings were immediately funneled to his wife.

The real focus of Marge's work was with the evening news. She worked tirelessly to improve the program with new sets and a new remote van that would allow for more local coverage. Along these lines she hired an additional reporter to handle the location work and the new look and content of the six o'clock news increased the stature and revenues of the station to the delight of her boss, the station manager.

San Angelo was a comfortable place to work and live; small, insular, and relaxed, and liking it that way. She loved her job and had settled into a comfortable routine when she met Steve George, a young Air Force enlisted man who was studying some sort of secret stuff at Goodfellow Air Force Base on the edge of town. He was a happy–go-lucky sort and they had a whirlwind romance that ended up in a hasty and secret marriage just before he was due to ship off to Alaska.

She could not go with him on his remote assignment but waited for him to return in eighteen months. Upon his return he told her that he was reenlisting. He would get a big bonus for re-upping and she would be able to travel with him to his next base in Germany as his wife after she was thoroughly vetted by the FBI. This was needed so as to assure the Air Force that she was not a communist subversive, a drug addict, or had some other undesirable trait that would leave her unfit to be the wife of a man who had a top-secret clearance.

She had a tough decision to make. Did she want to give up everything she had worked so hard for all these years to go traipsing off to Europe with a man she really hardly knew? She was not sure. So when her husband was assigned to another remote posting in Turkey where she could not accompany him, instead of Germany, she decided that his life and hers were too dissimilar to really be the basis for a strong marriage and that something needed to be done. She realized that their hasty decision to marry had been a big mistake from the start.

She was relieved but a little disappointed and her pride a bit wounded when he agreed to a divorce a little too readily. He went off to Turkey and from there who knows. She never heard from him again until she received the proceeds from a modest G.I. insurance policy of which she was named the beneficiary. He had been killed in Vietnam. She was shocked, saddened, and very ashamed. She had not even thought of him for years.

When she was sure that she was going to stay in San Angelo for a while, she found a small house to rent at the back of a large, imposing, Victorian mansion that had seen much better days. The immense structure itself looked as if it could have served as the set of the movie "Giant" if it had been located out in the open spaces. At any minute Marge

189

always expected Liz Taylor or Rock Hudson, or even better, James Dean, to come strolling back to her cottage to see how she was getting along. It never happened.

It turned out that her landlord, his wife and three kids who lived in the Giant house were in chronic need of money. They were the remnants of an old-time San Angelo ranching family who lived in town and had fallen on hard times due in equal parts to their unrealistic sense of entitlement, to the difficulties that had befallen the beef industry in general, to the drought-stricken state of their ranch, and to their poor management skills.

The upshot of this unfortunate set of circumstances was that they needed money and there was one easy way to get it without working for it. Sell something. They somehow, through pleading, or a little incentive under the table, or both, had convinced the town planning department to split off the rear portion of their huge lot into a separate parcel. It had the little house that Marge rented on it plus room for a garden, and her small garage with alley access. There was also a driveway easement from the street alongside the big house to her little bungalow.

Before the lot and house came onto the market she bought it. A local realtor who advertised on the station was also the person chosen by the family of the Giant house to determine the price. In the process of appraising the house for the purposes of establishing the fair-market value, he let it slip to Marge what he thought the house was worth. So just before the house came on the market she made a full-price offer to the eager sellers and they accepted. She made sure they paid the commission to the realtor. She had her own little house which she called "Jack" after the lad of beanstalk and Giant fame.

With ownership came a new pride in the house and she began a slow remodel of the entire place. She took her time and chose carefully and wisely the various elements of the new abode. In a year or so her little house was a showplace, at least to her, and was no longer deserving of the name Jack although a lot of just that had gone into her remodeling of it.

Her brother Mitchell and she had stayed in touch and he had written that her dad was sort of retiring and it sure would be nice if she could come home and pay a visit to the ranch. When she found out that Wes was back, living in town to stay, and most of all that he was still single, she started thinking that it was time to pay a long visit to her home. Although she was considered indispensable, she decided that she was going to use a goodly portion of the extensive vacation days she has accrued and take a month off and go to Montana.

When she has been home only a few days she ventures into town under the guise that she needs to shop for groceries but really with the idea of finding and confronting Wes. She goes up to his office about noon and finds that the reception area is empty. She marches right into his office.

"Well there you are; hiding out in your office. I've been back in town for three days and you haven't called once. If you think I'm going to chase after you like I used to then you have another thing coming. Those days are over. It's your turn to do the chasing. That is if you're interested. I'll give you an easy way to make up your mind. It's lunch time. I haven't had lunch yet. I bet you haven't either. What do you say? It's your first and last chance," Marge offers.

"Do you want to go to Luke's or Julia's? It's up to you," Wes replies.

"How about Julia's for lunch? And if that works out we can go to Luke's for dinner," she retorts.

"You're on. Let's go," Wes says as he rises from his desk.

Wes and Marge are seated in a corner booth.

"So here we are at last. You've got my undivided attention," Wes quips.

"It's about time. I've been trying to get your attention since I was a skinny twelve-year-old brat."

"Well you're not skinny anymore. And you might be a bit forward but you're sure no brat. All in all, I think you're just about right," Wes offers.

"Well, thank you I guess," she answers.

"So why did you go all the way to Austin to go to college? Was it for the music and BBQ?" Wes asks.

Marge and Wes have a pleasant time as she tells him about her adventures in Texas. It is a long and enjoyable lunch.

"I see that our waitress is anxious to leave so, if I pass the muster, can we continue this at Luke's around seven o'clock?" Wes asks.

"Oh you pass just fine. And I won't make you tell me all of your story. Just the details. I know most of it. I have spies," she replies.

Marge and Wes rise and head for the door. Marge turns and leaves him with a comment that almost makes him blush.

"I'll see you at seven and if that works out like I think it will, I might see you at the other seven...you know, the one in the morning."

That night they are seated across from each other at Luke's Grill. By coincidence, they are seated in the same booth he and Penny had shared on their first date. Marge finishes her story and asks Wes to tell his as well; which he does.

"I'm glad you came back," Wes says.

"Well I came home for a visit and to track you down and see if the old flame was still smoldering", she answers.

"And is it?

"No. It's not smoldering. It's hotter than hell. The question is how are your pyrotechnics doing?" she asks.

"Well to stay on the same metaphor. I'm ready for some fireworks. You lit my fire. Shall we see if I can light yours? "

"I've been waiting for this moment for a long time. The answer is yes. And watch out, I don't have a slow fuse where you're concerned," she states as they rise to leave and discover what the night has in store for them.

193

Three days before she is due to return to Texas she and Wes go fishing just upstream from the Clark Lodge on a warm and cloudless day. As they stand close to each other in their waders. He quickly moves toward her and, like Chris before him, trips on a rock, wobbles back and forth, and finally falls backward into the river. As he sits up in the water he has a look of awe on his face. He stares up at Marge, who is standing over him laughing hysterically.

"Will you marry me?" he blurts out.

Marge replies between fits of laughter, "Of course, I thought you'd never ask. If you'd waited any longer I would have had to ask you. I only have three days left of my vacation."

"I knew when you walked into my office I was hooked but I wanted to string you along and make you suffer some more," Wes says.

"Well I didn't suffer a bit. And I hope somewhere in the last few days, or nights, we've succeeded in creating another Wesley Felton so there can be yet another "and Son" on the door," she answers.

When she reaches out a hand to help him up, he pulls her down into the water on top of him and kisses her.

"How about a baptism before the wedding?" Wes asks as he kisses her again.

So they make plans to marry in a month. And Wes returns with her to Texas to help her move back to Montana. She sells her little house at a large profit, leaves Engineer Phil and her friends and co-workers at the station, packs up her belongings in a rental trailer and she and Wes strike out for the north. Another Feltondale vagabond headed for home.

Wes and Marge marry in September of 1965. Not long after, a barely respectable nine months, Wes IV is born and in twenty or so years, and the obligatory attendance at Yale, there hopefully will be another Wes Felton to fill the "and Son" spot on the sign.

Things are finally on course for Wes and Marge to have a complete and full life. All they have to do is live it.

CHAPTER TWENTY-THREE ... 1975, MONTANA

T he last ten years have found the town of Feltondale transformed; slightly in appearance; vastly in spirit.

The Feltondale Hardware store has gone through several significant changes. The annex next door is now fully part of the store and, in the spring and summer, displays a very good selection of fishing equipment and apparel. It does a brisk business in those items when the fishermen descend on the town each year from April to November. Sadly, the owner, Dill, died in 1969 one year after his sister Martha, but not before they saw their beloved Penny marry Chris. Penny and Chris now own Feltondale Hardware. Penny gave up her substitute teaching job, and helps Chris manage the store along with their assistant manager, Bill, who used to be called William.

Penny is deeply involved with Chris in the management of Feltondale Furniture as well. It has expanded to fill two large areas, one the original shop now owned by Chris and Penny, and the larger space next door on the alley that they lease. The shop is bustling with work orders from loyal customers from all over the country and, for that matter, the world.

Feltondale Furniture specializes in hand-made furniture following in the tradition of William Morris and the Arts and Crafts movement. Everything in the shop is handmade from start to finish. They have their own catalog of many types of custom-designed furniture, most with a rustic flair. They have developed several unique signature lines of furniture that include both Cowboy Chic and the National Park Lodge Collection.   They still make a line of Craftsman inspired Mission Style furniture and a very popular array of Country Oak items.

All the furniture is created by six full-time artisans trained by, and under the supervision of Chris, the hands-on owner. Each piece, being hand-made, is unique and is proudly signed by the carpenter. In addition to the employees of Feltondale Furniture the company is responsible for many other jobs in the area.

Early on in the furniture making process Chris had discovered the need for high-quality leather for seats and embellishments on his various pieces of furniture. He spoke with Mitchell Clark one day about the possibility of getting leather from the Clark Ranch knowing nothing about leather and how it is processed. Mitchell laughed and replied they might be able to think of something. Most of their cattle were sold on the open market after being trucked to the nearest railhead. When they left the ranch they were still alive and in need of their leather.

However, if Chris didn't need too much leather, the butcher shop at Hooker's Market bought a few steers a year and after the knacker man Jim Payson slaughtered and skinned the steers they hung the carcasses to age in their meat locker. Mitchell was sure Jim disposed of the hides. Chris should check with him.

Payson lived out of town on a small spread. He had a truck that he used for slaughtering and skinning the steers and delivering the carcasses to the market if needed. Chris asked what he did with the cow hides and he said that he generally just buried them. Chris asked if he could turn the hide into usable leather and Jim assured him that he could if he had the proper equipment. It was a messy process and required a lot of elbow grease and the use of some powerful chemicals but Jim was sure he could set up a tanning shop right here on his spread.

So Chris contracted for Jim to tan all the hides he could get his hands on. Chris would advance him the money for the tanning vats and equipment if Jim could guarantee a steady source of well-tanned leather. Another cottage industry was born.

In addition to leather, Chris found that he needed some fabric for his chair seats and sofas where leather was not used. Chris figured if he could get leather from local cows, then he could get wool from local sheep. He learned of a family in the area that traced their roots to an indigenous Indian tribe and who, besides raising their own sheep, spun the wool into thread, dyed it, and made wool blankets in the bright colors and designs of their ancestors.

Chris tracked down John Eaglefeather, the leader of this unofficial tribe, and set up a system by which he could order woven fabric in colors and designs that were selected by Chris from the many patterns that John and his weavers worked with. They had not produced much in the past as there was a very small local market for their goods.

Feltondale Furniture becomes a steady and reliable source of revenue for Eaglefeather Weavings. This is what John had picked when Chris suggested he should have a name for his works in order to promote them more effectively. Besides using Eaglefeather Weavings in his furniture Chris offers their products for sale to his ever-growing list of customers and there seems to be a great demand for the colorful rugs and blankets the Eaglefeather "tribe" produces. They have to expand dramatically. They have the sheep of course and the natural means to make more, if need be, and they train their whole clan in the art of weaving and somehow meet the increasing demand.

Another cottage, or better yet tribal, industry is added to the Feltondale economic mix.

Marge and Wes live in the Felton family home. Wes IV, who is now called Nate after the grandfather he never met, has moved into Wes's old room and loves it. Nate keeps his dad's old trophies on the shelf until he earns some of his own. Wes's mother decided she would like be a live-in Grandmother and babysitter, and she actually pays much more attention to little Nate than she ever did to her husband Nate or her son.

Wes's political career and unfinished plans for Feltondale are progressing nicely as well. He has finally won a seat on the Town Council after one of the stalwart members finally retires. Wes is currently Mayor of Feltondale as that mildly august post is filled each year by a rotation of the members of the Town Council. There are rumors that Wes might run for the state legislature and even try to return to Washington, D.C. to represent the district in the Congress.

An integral part of his political success he owes to his constant work to improve the economic situation of the town and the area. The Chamber of Commerce is a much more viable group than when he started it. They have championed a cause that resulted in changing the town laws to include rules about conserving the downtown in its present physical appearance and rigidly controlling commerce by only allowing retail establishments to be located in the downtown business sector. The economic base of the town has improved as well by the purchase and designation of a large tract of land in the southeast corner of the town for use as an industrial economic zone. This should help in future expansion. A company already has signed up to purchase a large building site on which they plan to build a plant to produce specialized home-gardening equipment.

They were referred by Charlie Childon who often visits his lodge and fishes with Chris and Wes.

With the continuing success of both Feltondale Furniture and the Clark Lodge which operates year-round and is highly regarded, things are looking up for Feltondale. The presence of the lodge has brought a level of consistent tourism to Feltondale that benefits the hotel and the new motor hotel on the outskirts of town that is owned and operated by the hotel. The influence of the lodge can be felt by the restaurants and other retail establishments as well; especially the hardware store.

Much more needs to be done to make Feltondale economically viable to the point that the flow of young folks to the city is completely reversed if that is at all possible. But there has been measurable success and the town is hopeful that there will be more to come if they are patient and at the same time active in their promotion of the town.

Wes Felton is considered a champion of the kind of controlled change that appeals to a wide political spectrum that includes both progressives and those of a conservative mind set.

CHAPTER TWENTY-FOUR ... 1977, THE PACIFIC

The brothers Daniels have become both famous and infamous throughout the South Seas for the high-quality output of their floating distillery. For the first time in their lives the brothers have salted away a somewhat sizable cache of money, converted by Mr. Wang into gem stones. This gives their fortune a portability that their precarious circumstances dictate is best in case of an urgent necessity to leave the scene of their employment.

It has been without the Captain's knowledge that they have secured with some of their profits, or wages of sin as they like to think of their moonshine money, their false ID's using the names of Charles and John Daniels. The Captain is also unaware of their stash of jewels and thinks that they are entirely in his debt and under his thumb. But they are not. And in some ways they are even rather cunning. They are aware that they are no longer needed to operate the distillery. They realize that they are now earning too large a portion of the profits and that the Captain would surely like to redirect more money into his own pocket. Their position is very vulnerable and they are aware that the profitable enterprise of the *Stella Stilla* might have a future, but they probably won't be a part of it.

In a small port on a remote island in Micronesia the brothers wander into a sailor's bar several blocks inland from the port itself. They are there to sample some of their own wares and generally let off some steam. It is strange that they need to come to a bar and spend good money to drink what they produce in great quantities almost every day. But the Captain has forbidden the consumption of alcohol on board the *Stella*. The brothers have an overnight here so they don't have to be home to the ship until sometime in the morning. They are seated on, rather less-than-sturdy, to down-right-rickety, bamboo stools in a remote corner of the bar.

Clarence turns to the bartender and asks, "Can you make us a couple of fancy rum drinks."

"How come you guys are drinkin' rum? Don't get enough of that stuff on board your floating still? How about some real whiskey, straight from the emerald isle?" the bartender asks.

"No. You've got it all wrong. We don't drink anything but water and coffee on board. The Captain's afraid that the crew will abuse the booze if we take even one sip, and believe you me the crew are poster children for abuse," John replies.

"Smart man that captain," the bartender offers.

"So let's make up a new cocktail. How about some guava juice and lime mixed up with our good old Stella rum and it wouldn't hurt if you could find some of those little umbrellas to class up this brand-new tropical delight," Clarence orders.

The bartender squeezes limes, purees guavas, and pours them with ice and rum into glasses and places them on the bar in front of the brothers.

"Here you are guys. They look kinda good. What do you call these things anyway?"

John takes a sip. "Don't know. How about a Stella Sunset? That sounds real sophisticated like them Singapore Slings."

"Yeah, that's classy. How do you like it?"

"At first sip this tastes real good but we need to know if they have lasting power. One is good sure, but what about ten? What will we think of them then? Tell you what, why don't you just keep making these *Stella Sunsets* till we tell you to stop."

Later that night after a monumental amount of *Stella Sunsets* the bar is almost empty but the brothers are still drinking. They have been joined by a smallish man dressed in black pants and a striped shirt worn by sailors of the French persuasion from Moorea to Marseille. He has a raspy annoying voice and he is carrying on about Polynesian maidens, sea shells, parrots, pirates, polyps and the like. The brothers are not paying much attention as he seems to fade in and out. Or perhaps the man is just slightly deranged or even completely daft. Whatever the case, his relentless patter seems to fall harmlessly into their ears and they pay him little attention.

"Can you understand anything this guy is saying? Sometimes he almost makes sense. I guess he's harmless, just a little eccentric as the Captain would say. Let's have another round of Stella Sunsets. We have to make a thorough test of their drinkability," Clarence says to John.

"Right you are brother the night may be old but the morning is young. But first, a visit to the powder room."

The brothers carefully dismount their stools and head out the back door. The minute they are out of sight the little sailor quickly becomes alert, and when the bartender has his back to the room, takes a small vial from the waistband of his pants and empties the contents in equal measure into the brothers' half-full drinks. The brothers return to their perch and finish their drinks.

Soon they are much more tipsy than the quart or so of rum they have consumed since arriving at the bar would call for. They slide slowly off of their stools and land in a big heap on the floor sound asleep. A short while after the beginning of their nap, three large men enter the bar from the rear door and, with the little French sailor, haul the brothers out the back door. They drag them down the alley and into a derelict building.

When the brothers awaken they find themselves in a dark room with pounding headaches and an awful taste like rotten bean sprouts in their mouths. But they immediately forget their physical ailments. They are faced with much bigger problems. They instinctively reach for their money belts under their

shirts and find them intact. But where the hell are
they? And why is it so damn dark?

They slowly and gingerly stand and walk a few
steps until they run into a wall. They turn right and
make their way along the wall until they reach what
feels like a doorway. They locate the door knob and
find that it won't turn. It is firmly locked. They are
trapped in some damn storeroom. They push against
the door and determine that it won't budge in the
slightest. They begin to panic. What time is it? How
long have they been in this dark hole? How did they
get here, wherever here is? Has their ship left? Are
they the victims of some sort of reverse Shanghai?

The only plan of action they can think of is to
apply some physical strength to the door until it gives
up. They put their shoulders to the task and start
pushing it. Nothing. So they back up and crash into
it. It gives a little bit. They repeat the run-and-smash
procedure until the door finally gives up and shatters.
Polynesian pine is no match for good-old Georgia
muscle.

Suddenly sun light rushes in to displace the
darkness and the boys are temporarily blinded. They
are free but sore.

They stumble out into the alley and begin running
toward the pier. They forget about revenge on
whoever locked them in that room, they just have to
get back to the ship. They pray that it hasn't left
without them.

Their prayers are answered by someone; the ship is still there but the mooring ropes are being untied. They've made it just in the nick of time. A few more minutes in that dark room and they would have had to take up residence on this God-forsaken island.

They scurry on board and head for their bunks to recover from their ordeal and somehow mitigate the painful residue of their debauchery and the beating they imposed on their bodies in the battle of the door.

CHAPTER TWENTY-FIVE ... 1977, MONTANA

T he last fifteen years have completely transformed Chris from isolated loner to productive, confident, creative, outgoing, and even intimate participant in life.

Some of this was due to his job at the Feltondale Hardware store; the first meaningful job he ever had in his life. He had learned and prospered under Dill's tutelage. He had become not just an employee but a partner, adding a positive new dimension to the store and relieving Dill from carrying the whole weight of it on his shoulders. They had had an easy trusting relationship.

Chris's friendship with Wes is another reason for his transformation. In Wes he finds both a best friend and a mentor; both of which are something he has never really had in his life before. He has always heard that, to have a friend you need to be a friend. But that is something that Chris had never been able to do; be a friend. Being a friend and having one is a completely new and sometimes baffling experience for Chris but he relishes and nurtures his friendship with Wes.

The third, and most important, component of his new life is Penny. Their courtship was a totally new experience for Chris. The intimacy of a growing romance had never been a factor in his life before. He was unsure of how to proceed but Penny seemed to sense this and made his stumbling advances easier and more comfortable as their relationship evolved.

But it was only after their quiet marriage that he really began to understand what being intimate was all about. Making love with someone you genuinely cared about was a new sensation for Chris; and in some ways for Penny as well.

However, it was the simple day-to-day intimacies that were a wonder to Chris. He had never shared his life with another person. There was never anyone who really cared about how his day had been when he came home. Penny taught him that he could trust and even express his feelings openly and not have to keep everything inside.

And he quickly learned that an experience shared was much more valuable than something you discovered on your own and kept to yourself. A life shared is a wonderful thing. And to Chris, a life shared with Penny was even more precious because they loved each other and she was, of course, Penny, who was really worth loving. There wasn't much more to say on that matter.

After their marriage they moved into Chris's small apartment. They had the option to move in with her dad but they felt that their privacy was an important factor in deciding where they would live. After all they were newlyweds.

Chris had kept his one-bedroom apartment. Though he could afford to, he never found a reason to move to a more expensive place. Penny had no objections to Chris's place. It was cozy and in many ways perfect for newlyweds who shouldn't yet feel that they each need their own space. That would come later.

Of course, Penny was given carte blanche by Chris to improve on his meager furnishings. She was frugal, but effective in making the place more comfortable, more tasteful, and much more livable. They would be happy there, or anywhere, with each other.

When Wes got married and moved into Felton Manor as his grandfather and father had called it, he offered to rent his little Craftsman bungalow to Chris and Penny for a reasonable rate. They moved into the larger home which seemed like a mansion after their little apartment. The home was furnished with furniture Chris had built. Living in a house where you had had such an important role in creating the overall ambiance gave him a strange but good feeling. Penny loved the house. She planted a garden and helped Chris convert the small garage on the alley into a full-fledged workshop and studio.

After he and Penny had lived in Wes's bungalow for a year, Chris accidently made an interesting discovery that launched his foray into the world of art. After looking at pictures of California bungalows that were very similar to Wes's little Sears home, he discovered that most of them had tile insets on either side of the fire box. Chris noticed that Wes's fireplace had no such decoration. He closely examined the fireplace and there were two places, right where the tiles should be, that were delineated by a rectangle of oak trim. Careful inspection revealed that the wood inside the framed space was different than the wood on the rest of the fireplace. It would seem that someone had taken out the tiles from this area and replaced them with little oak panels. Then the whole thing had been painted so they really blended in.

Chris and Wes had removed the paint during the remodel and the contrast in the oak was stark. It was a wonder to Chris that neither he nor Wes had discovered the mystery of the missing tiles before.

Chris measured both of the areas and calculated that they had each contained three four-inch square tiles. He decided to try and replace them as best he could, not by buying tiles, but by making them.

He ordered all the materials he needed to create custom tiles including glazes in the muted colors that were so popular with the Arts and Crafts designers. He had to order a small kiln to fire the tiles but he could justify the expense as he was planning to use custom hand-made tiles as embellishments on some of his furniture creations if these fireplace tiles came out okay. He decided on a William Morris plant motif for the design, and after a lot of trial and error, he was able to produce a very reasonable facsimile of the kind of tiles that quite possibly had been used in Wes's home.

He would successfully use this design, plus many others, in his furniture production and this unique feature was just another facet that contributed to the success of Feltondale Furniture. While it could be argued that these tiles were more craft than art they were the first step in Chris's fine-art avocation. There would be more to follow.

CHAPTER TWENTY-SIX ... 1977, THE PACIFIC

After their close call in the dark room the brothers are faced with a knotty problem. The question before them is simple. Just what the hell happened back there? It wasn't a robbery because they still have their money belts and treasure.

There are a couple of givens. They were drugged. It was probably that crazy little parrot guy. But the big question is why? And maybe who? Somehow they were lugged to that dark little room and left there to rot. Maybe someone wanted them to miss the ship. They pool their mental resources and come up with several scenarios all of which are possible and none of which are pleasant.

Who and why? Could it be that some local distiller or bootlegger who knew who they were and wanted them removed from the ship and by doing so damage the distilling operation of the *Stella?* That makes some sense; but not a lot. Maybe it was more straightforward and closer to home. Somebody on the crew? Only Manny could take their place and he wouldn't have had anything to do with their ordeal they were sure.

That leaves the Captain. That was a different matter. He sure seemed to make out like he was their buddy always looking out for them, but they knew at heart he was a slippery snake. Momma didn't raise up no fools. The Captain had just one person he was fond of; himself. Everybody else was either useful or expendable. It was as simple as that with him; and they knew it.

Maybe he was behind the whole thing. Maybe he hired that little weasel guy to put them out of the picture. After all he couldn't just throw them over board. The crew would be sure to notice even as dim as most of those rascals were. Kidnapping, like what happened, would be a good way to get rid of them without having to explain anything to the rest of the crew. But could the Captain be that low-down sneaky? He damn sure could. But they had foiled his little plan by making it back to the ship in one piece.

They arrive at two fairly sound conclusions. One, they'll never figure out what really happened no matter how hard they think about it. Two, maybe they have worn out their welcome. Maybe it's time to think about abandoning ship before the ship abandons them.

Could it be that it's time to go home? All the way home? Maybe so. This is probably not just an isolated incident. They better keep their eyes and ears open and not put themselves in a place where they can come to any harm. Maybe this is a good thing after all. Maybe it's a wake-up call.

They take stock. They have been quite successful and have lots of gems in their portable pouches. They were right in deciding to keep their false IDs and their little shore-side adventure with Mr. Wang to themselves. They were also right in thinking that they can't trust anybody but each other. They also realize that, except, for Manny, they sadly have only a few kinda friends, or better yet acquaintances, among the crew. They cannot really connect with any of them as they are, for the most part, from cultures that are completely alien to the homespun ways of the boys from the South.

And all of a sudden they become aware that all sirens do not reside in the water. The lure of land, and their rural childhood, is calling to them and they begin to realize that, at some time, they must return to America; probably sooner rather than later. So it would seem that they had better make plans to leave the good Captain, his rusty trusty ship, and his not-so-trusty crew behind them. As it turns out, the day of their departure is not so far away.

After stopping in Brazil for a short while, they are headed for a rare delivery in the United States. They are carrying a load of copra from the islands to San Pedro, the port of Los Angeles. Thank God it's not San Francisco.

The Daniels brothers decide to go on a toot in the Port of San Pedro and see if they are really ready to go home. How will it feel to be back in the USA? They soon discover it feels good. Nobody asks for their IDs and they seem to blend in real well; at least in San Pedro. It isn't much different than most any port in the world; just larger.

After surviving a set-to at the infamous Wilmington watering hole "The Nut House" they decide that being back in the states is where they belong and that it's time to jump ship and start up a new life in America. After all, it's just a matter of time before the Captain tries to get rid of them again. He is relentless when he wants something, or in this case, wants to get rid of something; namely them. They know that. It's time to go to the safe haven that they are sure awaits them somewhere back in Georgia.

When they return to the ship to gather their few belongings and to sneak off in the dead of night, they are shocked to find the ship has left without them. It seems their decision to abandon the floating distillery business was mutual.

Since they always have their fake ID's and their precious hoard of stones safely on their persons, the loss of the rest of their meager possessions really doesn't matter. So they head back into the big city to see how the country has gotten along without them

While having a celebratory beer or four at a local drinking establishment in Long Beach they make the acquaintance of a rather rough-and-tumble gentleman who reminds them in some ways of the Captain. He is the boss of a carnival however, not a ship. The carnival is a small, shabby, outfit that caters to small towns or sets up in the less-desirable outskirts of big cities. They have a variety of rides and games and an old-time carnival tent show that features *Danielle the French Contortionist* and a sword swallower who doubles as a fire eater.

All-in-all it is a rather sorry and sleazy operation that seems to be on its last legs. But it has been in that state for a number of years. There must be a sufficient number of low-brow customers that appreciate their sort of down-scale appeal.

The carnival is getting ready to pull up stakes and must begin their long trek eastward to return to their winter headquarters in Florida. And just like the circumstances years ago when they first came in contact with the *Stella*, it appears that the *Jessie Brothers Carnival* is short two roustabouts. They seem to have lost two unreliable employees to the mixture of alcohol, fisticuffs, and the local authorities.

The brothers think about this mode of travel. Is it a good idea? They could just take a bus across the country but that sounds like it would be no fun at all. A carnival might be a hoot and it would let them get reacquainted with their home country at a leisurely pace. And after all, some people have considered the boys to be clowns, so why not join the circus? If they keep their noses clean and stay out of trouble they can travel all the way to Georgia under the radar of anyone who may be looking for them if they are still being sought by the powers-that-be. Would the boys be interested? You're damn sure they would be.

So they begin a journey across the states learning to appreciate all they have missed in the last twelve years roaming around the Pacific. Their travels begin along the fabled Route 66. Their route is a reverse of the Bobby Troup song of the same name except they "forget Winona" and turn south at Flagstaff and head for Phoenix. There they turn east again to El Paso and move from small town to small town across Texas which seems to take forever. It is so large that it might as well be a separate country; and in some ways it is. They cross into the non-cowboy Deep South and finally after three months on the road arrive in Georgia.

According to Mr. Wang's list, the nearest place to home that they can exchange their jewel collection for cash is in Atlanta so they say goodbye to the carnival folks and head there by bus to locate Schmidt and Sons, wholesale jewelers in the center of the downtown area.

This is the big test. Will Mr. Wang's gems pass muster? Will Schmidt and his sons, steal them blind? Will they call the cops on them and keep the jewels? These are all questions that have crossed their minds. They are therefore very nervous as they enter the front door of the establishment. But they needn't have worried; Mr. Wang's letter opens the door wide for them.

The brothers are comfortably seated around a large oval table in a private room. They are treated with kindness and respect. Mr. Wang apparently carries a lot of weight even this far from Bangkok. Each one of their jewels is carefully examined and a tally of value is made. When the last jewel is liberated from their pouch and the tally totaled they are pleased to find that the actual worth of their treasure hoard is even higher than they had thought. If they don't spend the money like complete fools, they are set for life. But it has to cover them all the way to the grave. They are not likely to be applying for Social Security; they don't really exist.

Mr. Schmidt explains that over the years the value of many of the gems has increased and they are to reap the benefit of this pleasant phenomenon. Mr. Schmidt the elder gives them a company check for the entire amount and then explains that for their own protection they should not change this into cash but suggests that he will take them to his bank where they can get cash or a cashier's check for the full amount and deposit in their bank account.

Who wants a bank account? A bank account is something they have never had in their life. They rob banks don't they? Mr. Schmidt assures them that if they are really worried about having a bank account they can merely cash their cashier's check, rent a safety-deposit box, and store the money safely in that. Sure, they know banks get robbed, but they've gotta be a lot safer than any kind of Georgia mattress.

The boys opt for cash and they fill their empty money belts, and proceed to the hills of home. They know that they can't actually go home. There might be people looking for them there, so they settle down in a spot that is secluded and far enough from their real home so as not to be recognized. They get a safe deposit box at the local bank and fill it with cash.

And for the most part, they are happy and content. They buy a small house out in the boonies with a garden where they can get fresh vegetables all the time. And they raise a few pigs as well. When they run out of money they simply go to town, grab some cash from their safe-deposit box, and stop in at their favorite suds shop and have a few beers.

Life is good; that's for damn sure.

CHAPTER TWENTY-SEVEN... 1979, MONTANA

The whole world watches Chris's past life on the big screen and his new life is threatened. The movie "Escape from Alcatraz" comes out and it is as if the past Chris he has worked so hard to suppress and atone for comes rushing back. Chris is terrified. He knows he is going to be caught. Now everybody knows who Frank Morris is. Frank is resurrected and Chris is crucified.

It is all that Chris can do to go see the film when it comes to the Rialto. He sits in the dark theater in a state of shock. It is his story. Right here. Larger than life. As the credits are running at the end of the movie he has to make a conscious effort to get up and go out and face what he is sure a crowd of people looking at him. Thank God Penny had not wanted to come with him. She would have seen right through his efforts to remain calm and collected.

As he leaves the theater he is shocked that no one pays any untoward attention to him. Friends say "Hi" and he smiles and says "Hi" in return. But inside he is a mess.

He doesn't sleep well that night and shows up to work still in a state of apprehension.

Dill walks up to where he is working on a display of power tools.

"Did you see that new movie, 'Escape from Alcatraz'? It's a real nail biter. That Frank guy was a genius the way they got out of there," Dill remarks.

Chris is slow to answer. "Yeah, I saw it. Clint Eastwood was great but I thought parts of it were a little far-fetched. Like that old guy chopping off his fingers with a hatchet. Why would they have a hatchet in a wood-working shop; especially in a prison?" Chris replies.

"Do you think they got away?" Dill asks. "I was sort of pulling for them in the movie."

"No, no way. The current would be too strong and the water too cold. And the clincher is that all of the authorities from the FBI on down never found a trace of them, except that make-shift raft they found on Angel Island. No, they're dead for sure," Chris is almost adamant in his retort.

"Yeah, I guess you're right. But somehow I'd like to think there is a sliver of chance they got away. Especially Frank, he was the smart one. He might have made it."

"If he made it he'd be laughing about now," Chris offers.

But Chris is far from laughing. He is scared as hell. He finds out there is a book that the movie is based on. He has to find a copy but he can't ask the local book store. So he drives to the nearest big city and luckily finds a copy of "Escape from Alcatraz" by

J. Campbell Bruce. The very book the movie was based upon. Chris opens the book to the picture gallery in the center on the last page of pictures there he is staring out of the pages. The man he has tried so hard to erase all these years…Frank Morris with a sign around his neck:

U. S. Penitentiary

AlcatraZ

1441

1 20 60

Chris slams the book shut, carries it up to the cashier and buys it. He reads some of it in the car. He doesn't want to take any chances so he reads it at the shop after hours. It is a good book and very accurate. Hopefully nobody he knows will buy the book.

He keeps waiting for the axe to fall. But it never does. And after a while he kind of gets used to the idea that he and Clint Eastwood have something in common. They both used to be Frank Morris.

CHAPTER TWENTY-EIGHT ... 1981, MONTANA

Penny and Chris had lived in Wes's craftsman bungalow there for almost four years when Penny's dad Dill passed away.

Penny inherited the house in which she had been raised. It was a much larger home than the bungalow and there was never a question of them not moving into it. They loved the little bungalow but now they had their own place with no payments to make, and a free hand in fixing it up just the way they wanted it.

This move resulted, among other things, in a much bigger studio for Chris. There was a good reason for the ever expanding size of his studios; he really put them to good use. This had to do with another important element in Chris's growth; one that was more abstract than his interpersonal relationships but ultimately just as important. He had discovered he had a love and a passion for art.

Chris had always had the ability to use art for his own practical purposes. He could instinctively draw, paint, and sculpt with ease but until he came to Feltondale his artistic efforts never involved art for art's own sake; only for Chris's sake. This changed with a set of Arts and Crafts style tiles he had created for Wes's fireplace. This was the first step in his art avocation.

The second step involved Chris's introduction to the world of painting. He purchased a dusty set of Windsor Newton watercolors and brushes from the Barton-Colby variety store on Main Street. They also had a large stack of watercolor papers and he bought them all. He began to practice the basics of water-color painting from a book he checked out of the library that covered water colors from A to Z. He was soon proficient in water-color techniques from creating color washes to drawing fine lines with a rigger brush.

He had a book on fishing that Wes had given him one Christmas and it was illustrated with anatomically correct sketches of a variety of American fresh-water fish. He used these color sketches as a basis to create a set of six water colors of various types of trout in their native streams with western American scenes in the background. Some of the trout were leaping out of the water after flies, artificial or not, and several of them were in streams flashing their colors underwater. The results were quite impressive for a beginner, or even an expert for that matter. Penny hung them all around and was delighted that their house had turned into a fresh-water aquarium; after all they really were quite good, and more importantly, her husband had created them.

But the fish were destined for much greater exposure. One fall, when Charlie Childon was visiting their house after an enjoyable day of fishing he noticed the paintings and was immediately enthralled.

"Where did you get these wonderful watercolors, they are quite magnificent?" he inquired. Chris had to admit that he had painted them, though with some embarrassment. Charlie almost demanded that Chris make a limited edition of five sets of the series; one for every room in his lodge. Chris had no idea how to reproduce watercolors, especially here in this part of Montana so he painstakingly created thirty separate originals of the series.

Charlie was thrilled with the results and had them nicely done up in rustic frames. He insisted on paying for each one as if it were an original, which of course it was. He also asked if he could reproduce them and sell them in the lodge gift shop with royalties to Chris who gave his permission with some unexplainable reluctance that went beyond modesty. But he finally agreed to number and to sign them. This was really the sendoff of Chris's art career.

The third step was a big project Chris took upon himself. It was much more monumental, complicated, and daunting. In his voracious appetite for books and art it wasn't strange that he began to collect art books. One such book had a section on *trompe l'oeil* murals from the Baroque to the present day. *Tromp l'oeil* he learned, is French for "trick the eye". The murals of this type that intrigued him the most were the life-size depictions of illusionary space like false rooms that appeared so real that they did indeed trick the eye.

226

The spaces were filled with realistic imagery of the artist's choosing. As long as the items depicted in the illusionary space were realistically painted and were in the correct proportion, suitably becoming smaller as they moved into interior space, then they added to the sense of reality by actually heightening the illusion.

Chris was fascinated. He just had to try to create a mural like that. Somehow he just knew that he could accomplish the task. The first thing he had to do is find a suitable wall. It took a while but it turned out that his wall was right in front of him every day. The side wall of the hardware store that ran down Taylor Street had no windows or doors. It was a solid brick wall from Main Street to the alley. Brick of course is not a good surface upon which to paint. He had to think of a way to be able to create an illusion on the side of the building without directly putting paint on it. He mulled over the problem and finally came up with a solution when he noticed a piece of newspaper that a gust of wind had blown up on to the side of that very same wall. It looked like a white window and gave Chris the inspiration on how to make his mural on the brick wall.

He would paint it, not on paper, but on a strong surface like marine plywood and affix it to the wall. He would create two windows high-up on the wall where the second story was. He would create a third false window on the street level. This would be a large imaginary plate-glass window.

227

He first tested his idea with a mock-up of one of the smaller windows. He took an eight-by-four foot sheet of plywood with the long side on the bottom and the top, and attached a two-foot wide shutter on each end. This left a four-by-four foot section in the middle for the imaginary window. He drew some curtains on the plywood and then attached a window frame in this section. He set it up in his shop and it looked fairly real, but not very interesting; more of an architectural embellishment than art. He had to come up with something more thought-provoking in the window frame than just curtains. He had to paint something really striking to draw attention and cause interest. He tried several static arrangements and they just didn't seem right. He couldn't think of anything really appropriate until one day he saw a painting of Wes's grandfather in the law offices. That was it. He had found it. He would paint the old man in his stilted finery. The founder of this town would appear as if he were standing in the window looking out on the town he created, like a sentinel or a parent. Chris would paint him just as he stood in the formal portrait but with his hand on the top of a small occasional table as one would find in a bedroom. His gaze would be focused on Main Street as if he were surveying his domain and the stoic, expressionless, look on his face would not reveal whether he approved or disapproved of what had happened to his town; as if the jury was still out. He was a lawyer after all. He should be used to that.

Now, what about the other window; who could he put up there? In a moment of inspiration, he asked Penny if she had a picture of her grandfather. She searched through a box of old photos and found what looked like a Daguerreotype from the Civil War with a young man standing by an urn in a rigid pose. This was Dill's father in his early twenties. It would do nicely. Chris would pose him in the same manner as Wes's grandfather but looking downward toward his store and with a smile of approval on his face as he surveyed his hardware domain.

For the large store window on the first floor he decided to paint the inside of the hardware store as it would have looked if there were a real window there. But just for fun, and in keeping with the two windows above, he would paint the store as he imagined it would have looked way back then when it first opened with products that were more suitable to that time than the modern items they sold today; like plows and buggy whips.

It took a long time and a lot of sketches to come up with a painting that would fool anybody's eye for even a second. But he finally came up with one that he figured would do the job nicely. He had rendered the old store complete with shadows and the correct perspective which he had to learn from a "How to Draw in Proper Perspective" book he ordered from a mail-order catalog. He built a window frame around the edges of the faux window. The finished product would look like a real plate-glass window.   It took both Chris and Wes and two tall ladders to affix the two upper-floor windows to the wall. They had to suspend each window from the roof by ropes and then wrestle it into place and bolt it to the wall with the bolt heads countersunk behind where the shutters went. They installed the shutters last using galvanized screws.

The lower large window was harder to affix but easier to handle as it was on ground level. They bolted the wooden painting on the brick wall and covered up the countersunk bolt heads with matching paint.

From a proper distance there was nothing in the murals that, at first glance, would make them seem like anything but windows. At second glance, when the old men were discovered in the upper windows, and you noticed that the lower window revealed goods from a different era, there was a jolt of surprise mingled with a sense of discovery. People love to be fooled, especially when they get the joke.

The installation took place late on a quiet Sunday evening and when the street filled with people on Monday they were astonished, curious, and pleased to find this intriguing addition to their town.

As a result of this mural Chris was inundated with requests to do something like that for the other buildings in town. He politely turned them down. But when Karen Luebbers, the art teacher at the high school approached him with a request to help her with a project she was working on he could not refuse.

She wanted Chris to help her and her students create a mural on the high-school-gym wall that would be historical in nature dealing with the growth of the school from a one-room school house to its modern–day configuration. And of course it would have to include the Cougar mascot somehow. So he helped where he could. He let them figure out the design and had them make a large color mock-up of what it would look like in scale. He tweaked it here and there to make sure it had believable perspective. He then showed them how to draw a life-size sketch of the mural on the target wall by drawing a grid on the sketch and duplicating that grid on the wall that turned out to be thirteen times bigger than the one on the sketch. Then they drew the outline of the sketch in the big grid boxes on the wall. They used black charcoal for the outlines. Chris mixed up multiple pots of acrylic paint for each color that was to be used in the mural. There were more pots of the most popular colors. Then he made many Xerox's of the sketch and painted in the colors. On the big day the students climbed up on the scaffold with their pots of paint and a color sketch of the area they were working on, and filled in the colors like a big "paint by the numbers" set.

The kids had a great time and the results were laudable. It really dressed up the gym and with the original sketch being done by the most accomplished and talented artists in the class it was quite professional. They all signed the wall.

The history written on the wall told the story of education in the town in an easy-to-assimilate manner; sort of like a stained glass window in a church but without the religious overtones.

There were other mural projects that came along and Chris always lent a hand in the planning and execution but insisted that he take no credit for it. It was as if he didn't want anyone to know how talented he was.

A final creative flair that Chris developed was musical. There was an old piano that Penny had used when she learned piano fundamentals as a little girl. Chris found Penny's old elementary piano book in the piano bench one day. He dutifully played "My Little Sheep" and the other inane selections usually reserved for five-year olds. He learned to play well enough to amuse himself and even do some jazz improvisations from time to time. He also liked ragtime even though the syncopated rhythms sometimes drove him crazy. He could hear them, but they were difficult to play.

Penny was amazed at his seemingly innate musical ability and asked him if he had taken lessons before. He gave one of the terse answers that he always gave when anyone asked about his past.

"I played a little accordion, but I was never any good."

CHAPTER TWENTY-NINE ... 1982, MONTANA

One March day, when the river is raging at flood level, a car driven by a tourist, and containing her three small children, blows a tire and careens into the raging current.

Fortunately for her, Chris is on his way out to the Clark Lodge and witnesses the accident. It appears that the car is rapidly sinking and no one inside is able to get out. Without assessing the risks Chris throws his jacket to the ground and dives into the river. Several passersby watch as he succeeds in breaking the front passenger window of the car and extracting all of the passengers. He passes them back to a line of other rescuers that have strung themselves out into the river in order to create a human chain. When Chris reaches the shore he dons his jacket and drives off as if he is desirous of remaining anonymous; which he is.

But that is not the end of the story for him. The local TV station in the city forty miles to the north is made aware of the heroic rescue and sends a TV crew to Feltondale. They interview the grateful survivors, and discover the name of the reluctant hero; the mystery man who had saved the day.

It is too late in the day, they conclude, to interview him at the hardware store where he works so they proceed directly to his home in the waning hours of daylight. As they pull the TV van in front of the address they were given, they see a man scurry into the house from his seat on the front porch.

After repeated knocks upon his door he reluctantly comes outside on the porch and tells them that he only did his duty and there is nothing else he has to say, now, or in the future. With that terse statement he abruptly ends the short interview, turns and enters the house, and closes and locks the door.

But they have enough to stitch together a human-interest story that includes photos of the accident site, the interviews of the survivors, and the short statement that they caught on film on the hero's front porch. They have a great shot of him as he turns and momentarily faces the camera. It is a good piece and is picked up by their network for national release. It is carried on all of their affiliates as a bit of good news nestled in the intense coverage of the disasters de jour.

CHAPTER THIRTY ... 1982, GEORGIA

L ife continues on an even keel for the brothers. They are happy, and they still have plenty of cash in their safety-deposit box.

One day, after a visit to their cache at the bank where they retrieved some spending money, they stop in a small bar in town for a cold one, or two, or three. They are watching the news on TV with one eye, and little attention when a human-interest story is presented. They see a woman and some kids in a town out west being interviewed by a lady with a little red scarf and big hooters. The hooters capture their attention right away and they watch the screen with great interest.

As the reluctant hero of the piece tells the reporters to buzz off he turns to go inside but his face is clearly caught by the camera if just for a moment.

The brothers both gasp in unison, "By God that looks like Frank!"

Without a moment's hesitation they decide to take a trip out west to see if it really could be him. But they'll have to wait a month to make sure their garden is up and running.

Unfortunately for Chris, the reformed Anglin brothers are not the only unsavory characters from his past that recognize him from the brief TV story about the river rescue. There is one other person. And this person is much more dangerous. He could destroy Chris and the new life he has so painstakingly built.

CHAPTER THIRTY-ONE ...1982, MONTANA

After seeing himself on television Chris is somewhat worried about someone recognizing him. His transformation has been so complete that he has successfully shoved his past life into the furthest recesses of his consciousness. But now his past comes rushing back. It is as if he had just escaped. He realizes just how fragile his new existence really is. But there is nothing that he can do about it except to stay alert to anything that seems suspicious. He also checks as best he can to see if there were any reactions to the rescue story. There seem to be none that he can tell. But he doesn't want to draw attention to himself so his inquiries are very shallow.

After a while his worries begin to subside. He figures the chances of being recognized are slim. He hopes the years have changed his physical appearance as much as the inner aspects of his life. Still, he keeps his guard up and tries to maintain his edge by watching for any strangers in town or any unusual activity.

One day he sees a stranger about his age coming out of Smiley's bar. When the fellow notices Chris he seems flustered and turns back into the bar. Odd but not unheard of in the world of day drinking. Chris doesn't recognize him at all, but he notices him about town several other times. He seems to always appear in places where Chris frequents. Chris notices him on the street in front of the hardware store looking through the window. Chris is having lunch at Julia's and the fellow saunters past the window. One night Chris even discerns what seems to be someone standing in the shadows beyond the range of the streetlight across from his house. He can't be sure but it could be the same guy. Chris goes out the back door and around the side of the house to the street but by the time he gets there the fellow has vanished.

Chris decides it's just nerves but thinks that he'll keep tabs on this guy and maybe confront him. But what could he say? Any attempt to find out about his imaginary tracker might just cause more trouble than it's worth. Even after all these years he doesn't want to draw attention to himself. So he just watches and waits. After a while the whole episode seems to fade away.

But then one evening as he is crossing the alley between the hardware store and the furniture shop he thinks that someone is watching him from the shadows next to the loading dock. This is the last straw. Chris has had enough. He keeps walking nonchalantly down the alley and when he comes abreast of the hidden figure he jumps into shadows and grabs him.

"Who in the hell are you and why are you following me?" Chris gruffly asks as he drags his captured prey out into the alley by his throat. The man can't answer so Chris releases his throat and asks the question again.

"Who the hell are you?"

A sardonic smile comes across the man's face as he answers, "You don't' know me Frank but I sure as hell know all about you."

It is all Chris can do to hold on to the guy. He is in a state of shock. The last time he was called Frank he was swimming for his life with the Anglin brothers in the San Francisco Bay. This guy surely knows him. It would do no good to deny his identity or to protest his innocence. But the big question is "How does this guy know me? "He has never seen this guy before in his life. He needs an explanation. And fast.

"All right, I give, who the hell are you and how come you think you know me. No bullshit. Give me the whole story or I'll wring your neck right now. It's been a long time but I can still hold my own with a punk like you. Talk," Chris sputters in a rage that he has not felt for years.

"Ok pal. I'll give you the whole miserable story. My name is Steve Koyka and as I said you don't know me. But you sure as hell should remember the name Allen West. From Alcatraz? You betrayed him. He was a big part of the escape preparations and you just left him there when you decided to move up the escape date. He wasn't ready and you should have known it. The ventilator grill was stuck blocking his escape hole and by the time he got the grill, open you

239

all were gone and had taken the life raft with you. So
instead of escaping, he sat on the roof of the cell block
until dawn and eventually made his way back to his
cell. Allen told them all the details about the escape
plans, after all he was the mastermind. And he was
never charged for trying to escape but he was still
locked up. He never forgave you for ditching him.
He finally got out of the federal and state prison
system in nineteen-sixty-seven. But he wasn't free for
long. He was arrested in Florida for robbery and
some other stuff and sent back to the state pen for life.
That's where I met him. We were more than cell
mates. We were very close if you get my drift. And
he told me all about you. He had your picture on the
wall and he used to stare at it. He hated your guts.
Life wasn't easy for him. He was all broken inside.
There was a rage in him that I couldn't begin to calm.
He eventually killed some low-life boogy in nineteen-
seventy-two and they made life really rough for him
after that. They even put him in solitary for two
months before they sent him back to me. But our time
together was running out. One night he had a bad
pain in his gut and they took him to the hospital and
he died there. I bet all that hate inside he had for you
killed him. And I swore when he died that if I ever
found you I'd get even for him. But you never
surfaced. You completely disappeared. And then I
saw you on TV in that river rescue thing and I knew it
was you. I'd stared at your picture on the wall for so
long that it was part of me. I know you Frank. And

240

you're gonna pay for what you did to Allen," Steve says.

"You've got the story all wrong. He wasn't part of the planning and we didn't just desert him. Clarence tried to help him with the grill but it wouldn't budge. We had to go that night. We got rumors that they were going to move us to different cells the next day. We did all we could for him. We even left a small life raft, an oar, and a life jacket up on the roof to help him escape but it was dark and I guess he never found them. In the morning after the breakout the stuff we left on the roof of the cellblock was found by the guards. I know that because it was in the papers and believe me I kept close track of what went on after we got off that damned island. I'm sorry about what happened to Allen but none of it was my fault."

Steve quickly responds without much thought.

"You know Frank I don't care what you think about Allen. Or what happened. It makes no difference to me. The truth is that I have you in my clutches just like I dreamed about. And you can't get away. One word from me and your whole new life just crumbles. And you've got a pretty plush life here. I know because I've followed you around. You've done real well and it's about time you shared some of the gains you've made at Allen's expense. And since he's dead, in part because of hating you so much, I'll be the one who benefits from your treachery. You took Allen from me and now I want what's coming to me. It's only fair."

241

"What do you figure you've got coming besides a good beating?" Chris responds.

"Careful buddy, I hold the key to whether you live your live unmolested or go back to the pen. You've got to do everything you can to keep me happy and you know it. I've got you by the short hairs and I'm not going to let go. For starters I need some living money. I figure about ten grand should do for starters. You've got three days to come up with the dough or I'll give the authorities a little call and let them know the location of their most wanted fugitive."

Chris realizes that there are two ways he can keep his life together. He can pay this creep for the rest of his life or he can kill him. There are no other alternatives. Unfortunately, the man he once was, the man who could possibly commit the act of murder no matter how justified, is long gone. He'll have to come up with the money and then figure out if there is some other way to get rid of Steve and his sure-to-be unrelenting demands.

"Okay, Steve. I'll play it your way. I have no choice. Give me some time to round up the money. No matter what you think I don't have that kind of cash lying around idle."

"That's more like it Frank. I'll even start calling you Chris so there will be no mistakes on my part. I'll see you in three days. And as they say 'small bills' if you don't mind."

Steve strolls down the alley leaving Chris to figure out how he can get out of this mess without resorting to a violence he is not sure he can still deliver. He's got some time to figure it out, but not much. Maybe a miracle will happen, you never know.

CHAPTER THIRTY-TWO ... 1982, MONTANA

The next night, as if he doesn't have enough on his plate, a new problem arises. He is about to close up the hardware store. There are no customers left and it is time. Penny is going over to her book club tonight so he'll have to "bach" it. Maybe he'll just stop by the café for a bite. Not the grill, he's not up to all of that. He hasn't completely come to grips with the horrible turn his life has taken in the person of Steve the blackmailer.

He goes to the rear of the store to make sure the locks are secure on the back door. As he approaches the front door to make good his escape, he chuckles to himself about his choice of words. And then before him, looming in the doorway are two figures who have apparently risen from the dead. The one on the right confirms his worst suspicion when he simply says; "How ya doin' Frank? Long time no see."

Chris is speechless. After what seems to be an eternity he softly croaks, "My name is Chris."

"Sure it is. Chris is as good as any. And we're Charles and John Daniels. But the last time we saw you, you sure as hell was Frank, and we were freezin' our asses off. You remember that don't ya Frank? I mean Chris."

Chris feels as if he has been in a coma. And, maybe he has; for over fifteen or so years. But after the fiasco that Steve has created these two by comparison are a welcome sight.

"Sure guys, I remember although I must say I don't think about it as often as I used to. Come on let's go and get caught up. I'll close up the store here and we can go over to the furniture shop where we won't be disturbed; or noticed for that matter. Two large strangers in a town of this size will start the tongues to wagging and that wouldn't be a good idea for any one of us. We'll talk and then you need to get the hell out of here before we all get into trouble," Chris says.

And so they go back in the alley and Chris takes them to the furniture shop which is already closed for the night. They perch on three almost-finished chairs and relate their adventures.

The brothers tell their story. How they stowed away on an old tramp steamer, their adventures in the rum trade, their gem collecting, and their eventual return to the backwoods of Georgia. How they were a little taken aback by the movie and how they saw him on TV and had to check it out for themselves.

Chris tells them an abbreviated version of how he got to Feltondale and his life in the town since then, drastically underestimating his successes and making the town out to be less appealing than it is, in case they have any illusions of coming here to stay; or even pay another unwelcome visit. He finally tells them about the appearance of Steve and of his twisted story and his demands. He tells them that his life as he knows it may well be over but no matter what happens with Steve and his blackmail, the brothers will not come into the picture. Their secret is safe with him. They can go home assured that they'll not have to face any repercussions from his problems with Steve.

After having spent hours talking they all begin to realize that they had little in common back in the sixties except their mutual plight; and, despite their individual successes since then, that they still have little else in the way of shared interests. So after the conversation finally grinds to a halt, Chris suggests that it is time to part ways again; this time for good.

"It's been good to see you guys. I'd always wondered if you made it okay; and it sure seems like you did.   But before anyone knows you're here, I think it's time you head back home to Georgia and stay put. It seems you're safe back there, and I'll figure some way to deal with my current misfortunes. But remember, as Steve was happy to remind me, we aren't completely forgotten by the powers that be. So let's say you hop back in that car of yours and get yourselves gone."

They all stand up and leave the shop with Chris locking up after them.

"We're parked right out on the main street near the bar so we'll just mosey along then. You're right Frank, or Chris, we've found out what we came to find out so it's best we 'get gone' as you say. We're sure sorry about Steve and his lousy demands and we hope you figure out how to handle him short of getting rid of him for good. We'll send you a Christmas card to the hardware store here. Keep an eye out for one from the Daniels brothers and snag it before your wife finds it. See ya, Chris; and stay out of the water, you're pushing your luck." And with that they amble down the alley and out of his life. Almost.

Around three o'clock in the morning Chris is still downstairs unable to sleep. Penny has long ago gone to bed but Chris has too much on his mind to even think of sleeping. There is a soft knock at the front door and he leaps to open the door before Penny is disturbed. Standing on the porch are the Anglin brothers again. They haven't left town yet much to Chris's disappointment.

"Hey Frank, I mean Chris, don't get upset. We're on our way outta town but we just thought you should know what we've been up to for the last few hours. We were on our way home when we thought we'd stop at the bar and have a few good-bye beers. There was a fellow looks a lot like you said Steve did. He was sitting at the bar not talking to anyone and tossing back shots like he was celebrating something. We kept an eye on him and drank beer while we did. After an hour or so he got up and left so we left too and trailed him down the street. When he turned into an alley we decided to follow him and see what he was up to. As we turned into the alley he was waiting for us. He asked us why we were following him and we couldn't come up with an answer. As luck would have it we called him Steve and he didn't take likely to that. He asked us how we knew his name and we couldn't come up with an answer for that either. So we just told him we knew him from prison. That really set him off so we decided to shut him up with a few goodnight punches. That's when the shit hit the fan. He reached into his jacket pocket and came up with a little pistol of some kind and pointed it at us. Well that did not sit well. So while Clarence started to move to the left, Steve turned and I reached for his arm. We struggled for control of the gun and that's when it happened. The gun went off with a muffled roar. Well to make a long story short, you don't have to worry about Steve no more. He's no longer with us. Well actually he is, sorta, he's in the trunk of our car. We're on our way back home and we'll bury old Steve and his gun in nice deep grave somewhere along the way. Nobody will ever see him again and that's a good thing for all of us for damn sure."

"Let me get you a shovel out of the shed in back. I'll just take a moment," Chris offers.

Handing them the shovel, all Chris can do is shake their hands and thank them for saving his life. He closes the door and goes up to bed. Penny has not even stirred. He envies her ability to sleep through anything. Chris falls asleep quickly. There is nothing left to keep him awake.

Chris's life in Feltondale continues on its positive course. He often thinks of the brothers and how they saved his life but he rarely thinks past that fateful night to the life he left behind so long ago.

CHAPTER THIRTY-THREE...1983, MONTANA

Just as Chris has finally gotten over the scare of the movie, and the near disaster the TV clip brought him, another completely different moment from his past comes to town to haunt him. Maybe they're right. Maybe bad things do come in threes.

Chris is behind the counter at the hardware store when a middle-aged woman enters. She wanders around the store not seeming to look for anything in particular but glancing every-so-often at the front counter. As she is heading for the front door, Chris calls out to her.

"Is there anything that I can help you with?" he asks.

She turns slowly and comes up to the counter.

"Are you Christopher Stokes?" she asks

"Yes, but folks just call me Chris", he replies.

"Well, I'm Sally Draper but my maiden name was Stokes" she says looking directly at him.

"Oh, I see why you might be curious."

"I'm from near Salt Lake and I'm on my way to visit my daughter Betty. A friend of my daughter's said she saw a Christopher Stokes on TV who was from here and some sort of hero or something."

"That was a couple of years ago."

"Yeah, but I remembered what she said, and on

the outside chance that you might be my father, I came through Feltondale on my way to Spokane." she offers.

"So your father was named Christopher Stokes, too? Chris interjects.

"Yes, but I haven't seen my dad in years. He left when I was little and we barely kept in touch. The last time I heard from him he was in L.A. and he was real sick. I think it was because he had a drinking problem. I told him not to visit us. I didn't want my little daughter to be upset. But that's the last I heard from him. I'm sorry now I told him not to visit. Do you have any relatives in Utah? she asks.

"Sorry to disappoint you but I don't have any living relatives, anywhere. And I'm originally from back east."

"I guess I could have phoned but that would have been awkward. I've always wondered what happened to my dad. And now I guess I'll still have to wonder. I'd better get on the road while there is still plenty of light. Sorry to have bothered you. I'll let you get back to work."

"No bother at all. Too bad you had to take a detour only to be disappointed. Have a safe trip to Spokane. I guess you know the way," Chris says as she turns to leave.

"Sure do and thank you for being so understanding."

Chris feels bad that he couldn't explain that he'd

been with her dad when he died. But any closure she
would have gained by knowing her dad was dead
would have been offset by the mess it would have
caused in both of their lives.

CHAPTER THIRTY-FOUR ... 1997, MONTANA

Winter has taken its toll on a deserted city park at the edge of Feltondale. The grass is brown and the skies are gray. A light wind is testing the few leaves still left on the trees. Two old friends, Wes and Chris, are seated on a metal and wooden bench overlooking the park and a slow-moving river at the bottom of the hill. The river is spanned by a 1930's WPA concrete art-deco bridge that somehow is in keeping with its old-west surroundings.

As if the bleak setting encourages reflection, the men are reminiscing in muted tones.

"You know, Wes, we're way too old to be sitting out here in the cold. You'd think we'd have more sense," muses Chris. He is wearing a dark-blue watch cap and a pea coat as if he were a sailor far from the sea.

"We're here because we're creatures of habit. We've sat on this very bench in the heat of summer and the cold of winter for years. You're right though, it doesn't make much sense on a day like this, but you've got to take the good with the bad; that's what makes it a habit," says Wes. Since he has mostly retired his attire is more casual than his lawyer garb. He now just wears denims, plaid shirts, a well–worn brown cowboy hat, and a heavy green-twill jacket. "That was quite a spread the folks put on at your house. Have you eaten all the leftovers yet?" Wes asks.

It has been two days since Penny, Chris's wife of thirty-three years, was laid to rest in Saint Mary's Catholic Cemetery next to her father. Chris has gone through the services and the burial with a stoic certitude. After the interment everyone piled into cars and trucks, and returned to the church hall which was filled to overflowing by Chris and Penny's friends and neighbors. The church ladies had laid out a sumptuous buffet and there was enough food left over to fill Chris's kitchen and pantry with a month's worth of meals. Then the neighbors brought over another passel of home-baked dishes.

"It'll probably take years to eat all the food I've got stored over in our house. I think I could start a tuna casserole and Jell-O salad store. And my God, you won't believe the baked goods. I've got enough pies, cakes, and brownies to go into diabetic shock!" Chris confides. "I can't eat all of these goodies. It's been three days without Penny and I'm just getting a little of my appetite back. You and Marge and Nate will have to come over and help me with all of the foodstuffs," Chris says.

"I'll be happy to lend a hand and a stomach for that matter, but Marge is on another one of those diets so she'll probably pass up all the extra calories," Wes pauses and continues haltingly. "How are you doing

other than the food? You're probably lost without
Penny. I know, because I feel the same way."

"I'm sure you feel just as bewildered as I do Wes.
You and Penny were almost like sister and brother. I
know she felt that way. It's like she loved both of us,
but in different ways. I'm sure grateful I was the
husband and not the brother in that equation," Chris
replies. Wes feels that it isn't the right time to make a
comment and wonders if Chris has something else on
his mind.

After a long silence Chris haltingly reminisces
about his life with Penny in this small town that
adopted him years ago.

"It's been a good life for me here in Feltondale.
Until I came here I really hadn't lived at all. I was like
a blank canvas. Penny really painted my life for me.
But it wasn't just Penny. It was this town as well.
And of course the people in it: Penny's dad, you, all
of the folks. You all took me in, gave me room to
grow and let me live a productive and peaceful life.

And you know, I think that there's something
ageless and unspoiled about this place. When you
think about it, not much has changed since I first blew
into town in the early 60's. It's like we've all been
caught in a time warp; like Brigadoon without the
kilts and bagpipes," Chris muses.

Wes rises from the bench, "Come on, let's get out of
the cold before we turn as blue as Mel Gibson in
Braveheart, speaking of the Scots. Let's go over to

your house and see if you can find something for us to eat from your bountiful larder."

CHAPTER THIRTY-FIVE ... 1997, MONTANA

Wes and Chris are sitting at the kitchen table at Chris's house. They have just consumed a feast of leftover casseroles, salads, and desserts.

"I have a confession to make. It's time to fill you in on my life before Feltondale."

He pauses. It seems that Chris is reluctant to broach the subject but, at the same time, has a real need to speak of it. Finally, he gets the nerve again and begins. He speaks haltingly in a quiet and serious tone while Wes listens without interrupting, knowing how hard it is for Chris to reveal anything about himself. Chris speaks in a soft voice.

"I had two old friends from my past life come and visit me a while back. They had seen me on the national news when I pulled those people out of the river. They came half way across the country to find me and luckily they knew about the hardware store and went there first. Thank God Penny wasn't there.

We went to the furniture shop and they filled me in on what they'd been up to since we had last seen each other. They had left the country and made something of themselves even if only by somewhat questionable means. I listened to their story and told them a bit of my life here. I also told them about another person who came to visit me after seeing me on TV. This guy was blackmailing me and they got in a scrap with him in the alley near Smiley's Bar. He ended up dead when the gun he drew on them went off. It was self-defense and I owe them my life." So Chris begins his tale from the most recent part. Chris pauses and Wes asks a question to get him going again.

"So tell me why this guy was blackmailing you and who these guys were. I have a feeling you have a lot more to tell me; and now's as good a time as any. Continue with your story and I'll fill you in on my part after you've finished. I bet that this is going to be the longest you've talked since I've known you."

Chris begins once again. "Yeh, you're right. There is a lot more I need to tell you. Now that Penny is gone, I might as well get it all off of my chest. I guess I was scared to speak up before; afraid I'd lose this life I've built here. I could never tell any of this to Penny. At first it was because I was afraid of losing her. Later, I convinced myself that my old life was over and done with and to bring up the past would only cause pain and be of no earthly purpose. And that was probably true; then. Now with Penny out of the picture, I somehow feel that it would be best come clean. There is really no reason left not to," Chris says and then continues.

"I'll go back to the beginning. There's a lot more you need to know; and it's not pretty. Everything I've said so far about my visitors back then and what happened in the alley is true. But I left out the most important part of the story.

My unwanted visitors weren't old Army buddies. We were in the custody of the government but our uniforms weren't as glamorous as anything the Army has to offer, and they wouldn't even let us near any kind of weapon.

The three of us were on Alcatraz as guests of the penal system. Those two guys were in fact the Anglin brothers who had escaped from Alcatraz in the company of the ringleader who is sitting next to you at this moment. My real name is Frank Morris," Chris pauses waiting for a reaction. A slow smile comes across Wes's face. But that's all, he says nothing. Chris is bewildered.

"Is that all you're going to do is smile? I thought you'd be in shock. What gives anyway?" Chris asks.

"Well I'm surprised to actually hear it sure, but I'll fill you in on my lack of shock later. First of all, you need to tell me the whole story; about the escape and everything before that. You owe me that Chris; and you owe it to yourself as well. So let's start with the escape itself. That seems like as good a place as any to begin. How about that? Did the movie get it right, Clint?" Wes asks.

"Okay Wes, we'll play it your way. I'll tell you everything. After all you do deserve a full explanation. But when I'm through I want to hear all about why my confession didn't floor you. I thought you'd react a lot differently and there must be a reason," Chris says with a resigned look on his face. He gathers his thoughts and begins his story.

"So, you asked about the escape and the movie. Well, for the most part, the movie got it right. My only real complaint is that they made it seem easier and quicker than it really was. They sort of left you with the impression that it only took a little while to put all of that together. It really took around seven months or so to do everything we had to do to pull off such an elaborate plan. We had to dig through the walls at the back of our cells and camouflage it as we went. We had to make the rafts and life jackets. We had to make the faces out of paper mache and paint them. There was a lot of work and it took a long time. And a hell of a lot of luck I must add. Any number of things could have gone wrong in the process. We could have been caught at any time. It was a big gamble. But we won. And whoever wrote that movie, and the book it was based on for that matter, got it right," Chris said.

"Okay, Chris. Now tell me the story only you can tell. What happened after you guys got in the water?" Wes asks.

"Well first of all we got wet. And then we got cold," Chris says as a smile slowly appears on his face. "All right, I'm just kidding. I'll try and remember it as best as I can. And I'll throw in a few things the Anglins told me when they were here. But let me get through it all before you ask any questions. I can do it better that way. So here is what happened after I left the Rock right up to the summer day when I arrived in Feltondale in that old pick up and started my new life." Chris begins his story and Wes listens with rapt attention.

CHAPTER THIRTY-SIX ... 1997, MONTANA

Chris finishes his tale. "That's it; the end of the infamous escape from Alcatraz. The Anglins went out to sea and I came to Feltondale. But there is one other bit of luck that came my way. Dill thought that telling the town folks that I was his long-lost cousin, would make me be more readily accepted and make my job at the store easier. So I became sort of beyond suspicion. If I was good enough for Dill, then I was good enough for the folks in the town. Also, back then there wasn't much law enforcement in Feltondale; remember? The sheriff was up at the county seat. All there was in Feltondale was a deputy and lucky for me he was pretty ineffective. There wasn't much for him to do I guess so he just stayed pie-eyed or hungover most of the time. He was the only law-enforcement presence in town way back then and he probably never even looked at the wanted posters that were sent out by the FBI. They surely ended up in the round file. If he had been on the ball, and not on the bottle, he might have been suspicious even if Dill vouched for me. But he seemed to accept me as Dill's cousin just like everybody else.

I always looked over my shoulder and was suspicious of strangers in town thinking they may be looking for me. This well-founded paranoia lessened as the years went by. And I'm still here; an old man, sitting at my kitchen table with another old man and we are both stuffed to the gills. Now what about you? What are you hiding?" Chris asks as he finishes his account of the escape and waits for Wes to comment.

"Come on Chris, I'm not going to let you off that easy. I'll tell you my side in a while. But there's a lot more to your story than the escape and all. How in the hell did you end up on Alcatraz anyway?" Wes asks. "You know all about me; about my whole family. I never held back about all those Feltons. But you've always been the most tight-lipped guy I've ever met; so now's the time to fill me in on your life.

I'm your best friend and I deserve to finally hear what led you to us that summer in '62. I want your whole story and nothing but the truth; after all I am a lawyer. Start at the beginning and don't stop till I know everything there is to know about you and why you ended up on the Rock in the first place. I'll sit here quietly until you finish. You can ramble if you want, after all, no one but me is ever going to hear what you tell me. Go back to the beginning and tell me what it was really like to be Frank Morris. Where you were born, how you grew up, how you did in school; tell me the works," Wes says as he sits back and awaits the full story. Chris is slow to reply but when he finally begins his story just pours out; disjointed maybe but as complete as Chris's memory can make it.

263

"Honestly Wes, I really have kind of blocked out my past. I had to. I had to live in the present. The past had the power to drag me back if I let it. So I made a real effort to not let it slip into my consciousness. When it appeared, I shoved it back and concentrated on the present; and later when I could, on the future.

I never even told Penny about anything in my real past. And I trusted her with my life. But that was my new life; not my old life.

I'll try and fill you in on how I grew up and where I went wrong but you'll have to put up with some gaps and some sketchy bits. I'll do the best I can and I hope it all makes some sort of sense.

As I said, once I arrived here I never really took stock of my past life again. I guess I didn't want to face what I had done back then, so I sort of threw all the individual bad things I did into one big ugly pile where I could ignore them better. I'll try to separate them out again and I'll be as accurate as I can with everything I come up with," and with that preamble he begins his story.

CHAPTER THIRTY-SEVEN…1997, MONTANA

"I was born in Washington, D.C. I know that for sure. I've seen my birth certificate in the file that the social workers had on me. It was in 1926. Jeez, that seems so long ago. I must really be an old man by now.

So anyway, I don't remember much about my mother or father and I never have. My father was never there and my mom just didn't have a clue about much of anything. I guess she loved me as best as she could love anybody but, as I think back on it, she was just some sort of lost soul. When I was three or four she gave up on me and disappeared. By the way, when I was eleven I was told that both my mother and father were dead. I never shed a tear. Why should I? They were just two more adults who let me down.

So I was raised in foster homes from the time I was a little kid, until I ended up in the National Training School for Boys when I was fourteen.

I don't remember much about my early childhood at all. I just have a few images of pieces of my life and if I try to connect them I come up with nothing. I know I had some good folks look out for me. And there were bad ones too. There were hot sticky summers; after all D.C. was built on a swamp. And I remember very harsh winters with not enough to wear to keep out the bitter cold.

I also have stored in my memory, bits and pieces of attending school as a kid. I did okay some of the time but I never really connected with anyone, or anything. It's funny though, somehow I came up with a love of reading. I can't for the life of me remember if it was instilled in me by a teacher or a foster parent. It was as if it just happened. One day I wasn't reading, and the next day I was. I'm really surprised that I came to be such a voracious reader. I can remember reading all the time. Reading is escapism sure, but after all that's what I'm really good at. I took the reading habit right up to Alcatraz with me, where I worked in the library for a time. I guess I'm kind of smart; I know I pick up things quickly. And reading taught me an important lesson. I may not know everything, but I sure as hell know where to find out about anything; in a book.

My whole early life took place in the shadows of the Great Depression and that was a hell of a time to grow up even for someone with a strong sense of family and a stable environment. Without that you were toast. It seemed to me at the time that everybody was out of work. And you know you couldn't be sure that there would ever be any work again. The country was just sort of drifting or floundering. I know old FDR tried a bunch of stuff but none of it seemed to work.

I guess I figured out at an early age that it was just me. Nobody was going to help me or even give me a boost. I was on my own and I began to believe that I liked it that way. With a lot of time on my hands and a lot of needs that weren't being met, I started swiping things when I was still a kid. It was easy at first. As long as I stayed on my own I could manage and I never got caught in those days.

But I fell in with some older guys who were much bolder and, I see now, much more stupid than I was; less cautious and more daring. I swiped stuff because I needed it or perhaps just wanted it. They sometimes stole stuff just for the hell of it. Stealing got the adrenaline running.

Anyway, I became a member of what they would nowadays call a gang. We stole stuff and mugged a few older folks who were easy targets. The problem was that the people you mugged usually had less than you did. You can't get blood out of a turnip or money out of a pauper. We rousted some folks and got in fights with rival gangs that wandered into what we considered to be our territory. But you know, thinking back on it, I never felt that I fit in there either. I wasn't welcome on either side of the law. This gang was not my family. I didn't have one. So I pretty much stayed by myself. Even though I was in the gang, I was the quiet one. I was the one who clammed up and had nothing to say in the interminable bullshit sessions that went on between the various members of the gang.

If I had even once got my act together and tried to apply myself on the rare occasions when they forced me to go to school, then things might have turned out a lot better. But I never did. I was a loser. I just stayed isolated and alienated from everyone around me.

And soon I remember I got madder and madder. I began to resent everyone and everything. 'They', that was anyone but me, had stuff that I didn't have and I was going to get some things for myself without going through what normal folks went through. They were suckers. I always took the shortcut. But it always led to nowhere.

Then when I was about thirteen or so I got nabbed trying to steal money from the owner of a small grocery store. I got caught with my hand in the till if you will. And the judge of the Juvenile Court sent me to the National Training School in D.C. which is just another word for reform school, which is just another word for prison, kiddy prison ya, but prison nevertheless.

In this so-called Training School, I had a great job serving everybody else breakfast, lunch, and dinner. I worked in the mess hall and dished out the terrible food to the rest of the poor souls in that place. But they had to be nice to me because they thought I had the power to give them smaller portions or something. And besides that, I got plenty to eat.

Don't get me wrong, there was some actual training as the name implies. I guess I learned some things in that place. I was put in a trade class to learn how to be an electrician and that was great. I learned a lot and I was able to apply what I learned throughout my life in both good ways and bad. It really helped at the hardware store with the customers. I also learned a little math and English grammar in the mandatory classroom but you had to be careful to not appear too smart or to like learning too much, or you weren't tough and you weren't cool; and tough and cool were important.

But most of the stuff I learned was outside of the classroom from the other junior criminals I was locked up with. I learned how to boost a car and burgle a house. I was told how and where to find a gun and how to score illegal substances which were a lot harder to find than they are now. But believe me, the drug business is nothing new. There has always been an element of society that just likes to go around drunk or loaded. The usual drug addict is just plain stupid, but there are a lot of junkies who have a brain. They just need to escape living in their own skins for some reason or another; probably mostly due to the guilt of not using their God given talents which they are squandering using drugs. It's a vicious circle.

And I think alcohol and drugs play a big role in all of the crime that goes on nowadays. First, I think they are a major reason why some people turn to crime in the first place, and second, they are really a big factor in why most of them are such lousy criminals to begin with and keep getting caught. Another vicious circle.

Anyway I was paroled in 1943 and I graduated back out onto the streets. The war was still going on but I wasn't wanted in the service; even the Marines. My extensive but petty rap sheet and my time spent behind bars kept me safe from the bullets overseas. But it wasn't long before I violated my parole by simply not showing up when I was supposed to too many times. Wasn't that stupid?

This time I was sent away to an Ohio reform school in Chillicothe. It was okay but I wasn't there for long. I was paroled again. It was becoming like a revolving door.

Each time I got out I promised myself that I would keep out of jail. But I wasn't going to really do anything that would insure that I stayed out of the slammer. I was too smart, too cocky, too tough, and too much of a lot of things to stay out of trouble.

My life from that point on until I got to Feltondale was just one setback after another. And these disappointments were the result of my bad behavior. I was to blame. No one else.

I guess I was by then what you would call incorrigible. I did three years in Louisiana at the infamous Angola State Prison. And then I was in Raiford in Florida where I escaped. I was caught again and then sent back to Raiford. And then back to Angola. I attempted another escape in New Orleans where I was awaiting trial. Then I was sent to the U.S. Penitentiary at Atlanta after I broke into a FDIC depository. Most all of my crimes were burglary even the FDIC one. I guess I'm just not the type to confront people and try to take their money. I'm not really a people person. I'd rather sneak in and take it behind their backs.

But my bungled burglaries were not what got me into Alcatraz. I was sent to Alcatraz because of my ability to escape from ordinary prisons. They thought they could keep me on the Rock. Well I proved them wrong.

So there's the chronological summary of most of my criminal activities but that doesn't tell the real story. It doesn't really answer the question 'Who in the hell was this Frank Morris guy anyway?' does it. 'What made him tick?' 'And how does he relate to the man sitting here telling his story?' Those are good questions and are much harder things to talk about.

You know, when I think back to my earlier days it seems as if that person, that Frank Morris, was a totally different man than I am now. I've read accounts of the escape and most of the writers offer an opinion as to whether we survived the escape or not. A few say that the Anglin brothers died and I somehow survived. But most concur that Frank Morris died as well. And I agree with them. Frank Morris died during the escape. Maybe not on the bay but somewhere between the Rock and Feltondale he surely disappeared. Chris Stokes died too and was reborn as a man who looked a lot like Frank Morris but whose memory needed to be erased and become a blank slate, a tabula rasa I think they call it, ready to

271

be filled with the things a real human being needs to know; ready to take his place in society and be of some use to himself and others. That's something that the old loner Frank Morris could never have done.

Some of the explanation of Frank's bad behavior has to do with where he was raised, or not raised, as the case may be. Not an excuse but an explanation.

I've sometimes wondered over the last thirty or so years of what I would have been like if I had been born in Feltondale instead of a big city like Washington, D.C. Even if I had been an orphan I would have most likely been adopted by someone here and I would have been instilled with some sort of moral code and not just left to fend for myself. Also, I think you folks here in Feltondale must have survived the Great Depression in a better fashion than those folks in the big city. There is a close sense of community here and I bet if the folks back then, were anything like the folks who live here now, there would have been sharing and neighborly compassion; something that was totally lacking where I grew up. You would have pulled together. We just pulled apart.

It's said that you get a little sense of camaraderie in the prison or the reform school community. But it's for all the wrong reasons. It's an 'us against them' sort of mentality on top of an 'every man for himself' foundation that really isn't the same thing at all. That's not a real sense of community. It's one group, the prisoners, against another group, the guards and the society that they represent. Anyway enough of that mental masturbation; it really has never gotten me anywhere.

I was talking about my new persona; that of a prison escape artist. As I said, that's what landed me in Alcatraz. Not the so-called heinous nature of my crimes, though they were bad. It was the fact that I escaped so often that they felt they had to put me in what they thought was the only escape-proof prison in the system. Interestingly enough that's why the Anglin's were there as well. They escaped a lot too. They were really very clever at it sometimes.

It's funny, the only thing I did really well in my former life as Frank Morris was to break out of prison. The escape from Alcatraz was the crowning achievement of that dubious career. And I was kind of famous after the movie even though everybody thought I was dead. I always got a secret kick out of being portrayed by Clint Eastwood. I guess I fall somewhere between Rowdy Yates and Dirty Harry in the lineup of Eastwood characters but with one big distinction. I was a real guy not the fig newton of some writer's imagination. I think Clint did a pretty good job in that role. Perhaps if I had any complaints it was that he played me a little too tough and confrontational. I was always a little more scared and I tried like hell to be ignored by the other prisoners and the guards as well. But maybe I was just scared inside. Maybe nobody saw me that way. I have no idea, but anyway Clint did a good job. And the older

he gets, and the older I get, he is beginning to look a
lot like me."

CHAPTER THIRTY-EIGHT ... 1997, MONTANA

"Well that's about it, Wes. Thanks for letting me get it off of my chest without interrupting. It was tough but I feel better after confessing. Maybe I should have been a Catholic," Chris adds with a grin and makes his summation to the town's leading lawyer.

"So now you know the whole sordid story. And if your strong sense of justice prevails then I guess you ought to turn me in. You have every right and maybe even a duty. But I hope that you take into account all that I have become and how I have changed, living here over the years. Frank Morris really is dead but I would be willing to serve out the rest of his sentence for him if I have to. It's up to you. You are the best friend I ever had. Not counting Penny of course. But she is no longer here to watch out for me. So, as I said, it's up to you. Now, it's your turn Wes. Why weren't you shocked when I told you I was really Frank Morris? Did you know already? Have you known all along? It's my turn to listen; your turn to talk," Chris says as he leans back and awaits Wes's revelations. It takes Wes a while to respond.

"That's a great story Chris. You'll always be Chris to me. You don't even seem like a Frank or Clint for that matter. As you surmised I've suspected who you really are for some time now. It all started with that movie "Escape from Alcatraz" and really with the book it was based on. I saw the movie when it first came out right here at the Rialto. It was a favorite of mine. Over the years, I saw bits and pieces of the movie on TV. It seems that 'Escape from Alcatraz' and 'The Shawshank Redemption' alternate every week somewhere on one of those movie channels on cable.

Then I got the book and I read it through in one sitting. When I came across a gallery of pictures in the middle of the book, there were photos of the real escapees.

So anyway, when I saw the picture of Frank Morris, the third escapee, I thought the face was familiar. He looked remarkably like my friend Chris without the mustache and short hair. That's when I put two and two together and thought you might be Frank Morris. I was an elected official by then and I could have easily gotten some fingerprints and really made sure. But if I requested a fingerprint search of the Feds, bells would go off and they would be alerted to your suspected presence in Feltondale. They'd march into town looking for Frank Morris. They'd grab you and Penny would never forgive me for ruining her life.

And here's another shocker for you. You might have kept a lot from Penny but she kept a big secret from you. At least I hope she did. Penny might have told you but we swore to each other that we wouldn't and I've never told Marge. Here's the secret. Penny and I are related. I am actually Penny's half-brother. Her mom and my dad had a fling just before she married Dill. That's why I abruptly quit courting Penny. We share a biological father. And I promised her way back then that I would always watch out for her and I guess that included watching out for you as well, as hard as that may seem," Wes pauses as if to let Chris comment on this revelation. But Chris just appears sort of dazed so Wes continues.

"So I decided that justice in this situation would be best served by keeping the peace and not actively investigating your background. I was pretty sure it was you. I surreptitiously looked up the records for a Christopher Stokes and found nothing out of the ordinary. There was a vagrancy charge and a drunk-in-public, but that was all. Nothing that would make it seem that you were using a false identity. After all, there were no pictures or fingerprints on driver's licenses back then. After he, or you, arrived here there was nothing. But of course I knew that.

But after I thought you might be Frank Morris, there were other little things about you that added to my suspicions. Like your fascination with art and your ability as an artist. And once when I commented on how you seemed to learn to play the piano out of the blue, Penny mentioned that you had told her you once played the accordion a little. Those two things by themselves meant absolutely nothing. But then I read the book and saw your picture. I remembered how the movie showed Frank Morris painting the face

277

masks for the escape and using an accordion case to hide the hole he was digging in his cell. And then for a while after the movie came out you stopped painting and playing the piano. It seemed to me that you might not have wanted to be in any way associated with the fact that Frank did those things as well. A coincidence?

And like the fact that you always wear long-sleeved shirts and never wear shorts. I read in the book that Frank Morris had a tattoo of a devil on his upper arm and some little ones on his legs. And you had a large scar on your upper arm that I saw once when we were changing clothes after fishing. Was all of that because of the tattoos? Another little clue.

I remember the Fourth of July picnic one year. I asked you why you didn't cool off in the lake like the rest of us and you said you couldn't swim. But then you saved those people from drowning and I remembered what you had said. What were you hiding? A moonlight swim in the San Francisco Bay perhaps. Another clue.

But still I kept quiet for Penny's sake and also I guess by then you'd kind of grown on me in your quiet way.

You helped me improve this town, Chris, and you lived an upright life here and you are well respected as a member of the community. Far be it for me to disrupt the life you and my sister had created.

However, I didn't just ignore my strong sense of justice as you call it. If I couldn't turn you in and send you back to prison, I at least could be your local warden. You were still in prison but you just didn't know it. Over the years more clues to your identity came to light but I stayed with my decision and you never gave me cause to be anything other than a watchdog. Believe me, if you had stepped out of line I would have noticed, and your new life would have ended, Penny or no Penny, Chris or no Chris.

You might think that now with Penny no longer in the picture I might finally take some further action. But you know, after all these years of staying close to you and keeping an eye on you, I think I agree with you. Frank Morris is as dead as if he had drowned in the cold waters of the San Francisco Bay.

But maybe there's more to it. It's a little weird but maybe you are part of some grand plan. Maybe you were spared a watery death in the bay so you'd be around to take another swim and save that woman and those kids. That's all pretty off-the-wall stuff and we'll never know, but as to the woman and her kids, I'm sure they are quite glad you were around to save their bacon.

Anyway, I don't want to hear any more about your old life. To me, Frank's dead and Chris can spend the rest of his life knowing his secret is safe.

You know, I've rather enjoyed being your best friend and my judgment about people is always perfect. I'd never be a friend to the likes of Frank Morris. So I'm going to forget all about your story and your interpretation of your past. I suggest you do

279

the same. Let's go back out into the cold and walk off some of this food. We can get a cup of coffee at Julia's cafe and finally put all of the past to rest where it belongs. And by the way, you're buying; you owe me big time," Wes states as he starts to rise.

"Not so fast, Wes there's one more thing or maybe two. I am in need of your good services. Not as a friend but as a lawyer. Let me explain. I'm all alone now. Penny's gone. We were not fortunate enough to have kids; probably my fault. By the way, I can't believe we're related even if only by marriage. But come to think of it you and Penny are a lot alike. So anyway, the bottom line is I now have a lot of stuff in my life and no one to leave it to. And here's where you come in. I want to set up a trust of some sort and leave the furniture company and the hardware store and the house as well, to the people who really made them work; the employees and the people of Feltondale. I'll be on the board till I die. I want you and Wes IV, or Nate as he calls himself, to be the trustees as well, along with whomever you think should be on the board of trustees. When I die, you can keep the companies and run them, or sell them. That's up to you. But all the profits, or the earnings, should go to Feltondale, to the schools, or the parks or whatever you think should be the benefactors. Can you do this for me?" Chris asks.

"My God, what a great idea, of course I'll do it. It's funny I am the one who is always talking about increasing the economic base of the town and all the while you are the one who actually is doing it; first with Feltondale Furniture and all of its dangling affiliates, and now with this. You know, you're a real hero and I'd be honored to give you a hand setting up the trust and being on the board as a trustee. And I know your Godson will feel the same way. You've got Felton and Son on your team. We can make a trust in perpetuity that will benefit the town in immeasurable ways for a long, long time," Wes assures Chris.

"You know something Wes? You're too damn modest. You were always the General in charge of getting things done in town. You're the one who went to the state legislature and then on to Congress. I was just one of the boots on the ground. Big boots maybe, but boots never-the-less," Chris interjects and continues.

"And there is one more thing that popped into my mind, Wes. I've been thinking that I might write a book about what happened to me after I escaped from the Rock. I'd have to get hold of the Anglins but who knows. They shouldn't mind, after all, they weren't bad guys at heart; just misguided big kids really. The worst crimes they ever committed were their prison escapes. And after Alcatraz their adventures were rather harmless and really rather productive. They stayed out of trouble which is really all you can ask. And I think they had children and if they did, it would be nice for them to find out that their dads could be remembered as enterprising business men

281

and not as just unsuccessful criminals who were good escape artists.

Anyway, I'll think about it. Maybe if there was a book there could be movie too. Clint Eastwood would play me as an old man on the bench of course. Maybe the Quaid brothers could be the Anglins. Who would you want to play you?" Chris asks.

"Good grief, you're really on a flight of fantasy aren't you?" Wes quips. "But to your question, I guess I'd choose Clint's old buddy Tommy Lee Jones from 'Space Cowboys'. After all Gary Cooper is dead and so is Randolph Scott," Wes replies with a smile. "You know, the idea of a book? That's not so crazy. Why don't you write it Chris; you know the story better than anybody else and you have a lot of time on your hands now. You'd have to write it as Mr. Anonymous or the authorities and maybe even the Anglins would come after you. But maybe Clint would pick up the movie rights, you never know, "Wes concludes and starts to stand.

"One more quick favor, Wes. I want you to take a trip with me. Just for a short while. I want to go to San Francisco for a couple of days. There is a tour I want to take. You may think I'm crazy but I want to go back to Alcatraz; not to stay; just to visit."

CHAPTER THIRTY-NINE ... 1998, MONTANA

When they get back from San Francisco Chris is even more enthused about writing a book. He was kidding at first but the more he thinks about it, the more appealing it is. The story of his transformation from career criminal to respected citizen is compelling. And after all a book is just a bunch of words. How hard can it be?

But it is hard. He tries, on and off, for several years. He begins by changing all the names to protect the innocent. He does a good job of disguising Feltondale and all of the people in it. It's a tall order but he is pretty sure that no one will recognize anything. But the real problem is that he just can't write the book. No matter how hard he tries he just seems to make a mess of the story. He has the facts all right, but he doesn't know how to put them on paper in a way that is appealing. He may be a fairly accomplished artist but he is not a writer. And he realizes that no matter how long he tries, he never will be. He has hundreds of pages of notes and even some rough chapters. He has written what he knows of all of the major characters but it won't come together. It just doesn't work. He has a good story but he needs someone else to write it. And, when he thinks about it he can't really be involved in any way. Including the Anglins in the story might be a little iffy but if he doesn't give away their present location and changes the names of the other folks in their story they probably wouldn't mind. They'd get a kick out of it most likely. And after all, it's fiction.

Another reason he can't put his name on the book is that in spite of his camouflage efforts, somebody might put two and two together and come up with the name of the real town or one of the real people. There is too much to lose; for him and for the town as well. They would not be amused to find that they had been hiding a fugitive for all these years. It could offset all of the worthwhile efforts that have been made to improve the town.

Everybody thinks he is dead, so why not keep it that way. He can't write his book. But there is no law that some other writer can't write a fictional biography; an account of what happened to him after the escape. He is sure that somebody might be intrigued and want to take on the task, but the only writer he can think of who would really be interested and savvy enough do a good job with the story is the guy who wrote "Escape from Alcatraz" in the first place. Why not him?

He goes to the computer at the library to find out if the author is still alive. Alas, he died in 1995. But he has three children and the oldest is named Kevin Bruce and it says he went to Stanford and has a Master of Liberal Arts degree. As the Anglins would say, "He damn sure ought to be able to write."

Chris thinks about contacting him and making some sort of deal to write the book. But that won't work. All of the legal issues would kill the project and no publisher would touch it. He needs to stay completely anonymous.

So Chris decides to take a flyer. He discusses it with Wes who agrees that is probably the best way to handle the dilemma. If it works, then his story will get out, and no one will be put in jeopardy. He gets the address of this Kevin Bruce guy and packs up everything he has written, every scrap of information, his whole story from beginning to end, all of it disguised to protect the innocent. He will make the long trip to Salt Lake City and mail it to him with no return address.

"The final outcome is out of my hands. I've done all I can do to try and get the story told," Chris thinks. He experiences a mixture of accomplishment and release. As he drops his precious parcel into the "Out of Town" mail box at the Post Office, he murmurs a farewell thought to himself.

"So long Frank. Rest in peace."

EPILOGUE ... 2012, ARIZONA

I received the anonymous package in 2000. At first, I couldn't believe it. But as I read Frank Morris's story I wasn't so sure. It seemed to ring true. It was too bad that Frank Morris hadn't started this project a little earlier when my father was still alive. He could have written his book for him with ease. My father wrote the book *Escape from Alcatraz* and was a prolific non-fiction contributor to national magazines on top of being a distinguished newspaper reporter for many years. He was the real writer in the family.

I put the envelope in the top-drawer of my desk and forgot about it. It was probably a joke anyway.

Then, several years later, I received another anonymous piece of mail from San Francisco, this time. It was an Alcatraz postcard and simply asked, "How's our book coming along? Frank."

This card re-piqued my interest. I took the envelope out of my desk and went through it again. It was still very intriguing but the real question was still plaguing me; "Did that envelope really come from Frank Morris?" I finally came up with an idea that might answer the big question. If I had a copy of Frank Morris's fingerprints, I could check the mystery envelope and the papers in it for fingerprints and see if they matched. I checked on the internet for the FBI files from the escape. I found them and located on page 62 was a copy of the Frank Morris "Wanted by FBI" poster dated June 18, 1962 ID number 3584. On the poster were all ten of his fingerprints. From there on it was simple. I made some fingerprint dust from instructions on the internet out of starch powder and soot.   I sprinkled some of it on the pages that the alleged Frank had sent to me. I blew off the dust and there they were; fingerprints. Whoever sent the envelope had not tried to hide his identity from me. I compared them with the prints on the wanted poster and they sure seemed to match. At least close enough for me to believe that it really was Frank Morris who sent the story of his life to me; just like he said it was.

It was time I tried to live up to the faith Frank Morris had placed in my abilities to write his story for him. Somehow I thought I owed him that much. I finally got organized and again went through his writings, and the rough chapters that weren't really all that rough. I went through all of his notes, his anecdotes, and even his scribblings. Then I got serious and started writing. I made sure to use the fictitious town and people. And to tell you the truth I never could figure out where Feltondale really was.   Frank did a good job of being anonymous.

It took me a long time to write the book. I had never written fiction before and sometimes I didn't feel up to the task. But then the fact that Frank, or Chris, was counting on me, spurred me on. Thank you, Frank. I apologize for taking so long to get your story written. I hope you and Wes are still alive and enjoy how it came out.

And then finally, just in time for the fiftieth anniversary of the infamous escape, the book is published and Frank's story is finally out there just like he wanted it to be.

And you have just finished reading it.

And what about the Anglins? I hope Frank got their part right and that they are happy with the results. After all, it's not just about Frank. It's about the eventual redemption of all three of the participants in the escape from Alcatraz.

I hope everyone will come to see the movie, if there is one, and it would be nice if it's Clint and Tommy Lee sitting on that cold bench.

Kevin Bruce
Scottsdale, Arizona, June 11, 2012

Christopher Stokes, John and Charles Daniels
Whereabouts unknown

Frank Morris
Deceased.

288